Family Fallout

Family Fallout

Peter Conway

ROBERT HALE · LONDON

© Peter Conway 2011
First published in Great Britain 2011

ISBN 978-0-7090-9251-3

Robert Hale Limited
Clerkenwell House
Clerkenwell Green
London EC1R 0HT

www.halebooks.com

2 4 6 8 10 9 7 5 3 1

Typeset in 11.25/19pt New Century Schoolbook
Printed in Great Britain by the MPG Books Group,
Bodmin and King's Lynn

ONE

'HOPE THE DENTIST weren't too bad, Phil.'

'Just the one filling,' Mr Palmer. Sorry I took so long there.'

'That's all right, but make sure you go back there regular, like. You don't want to finish up wearin' a plate like me, do you? What took you so long?'

'Bit of a queue ahead of me.'

'Right busy day ahead of us and we'll have to get a shift on. I've just been down to the bottom of the lawn and some of the branches beyond came down in that thunderstorm last night. Happen some of them have fallen into the stream down there and we don't want it to get blocked. Start off by clearing 'em, will you, and then any that have fallen into the pool. There's a tidy lot of other stuff for your to do later, an' all.'

'What shall I do with the branches, Mr Palmer?'

'Better pile 'em up out of sight where we have the bonfire an' I'll sort 'em out later.'

Fred Palmer watched Phil Carter walk briskly towards

the trees. He was a good lad, he thought, unlike most of those of that age in the village, who spent a large measure of their time asleep, when they were not loafing around or getting up to alcopop fuelled noise and mischief. The girls were as bad as the boys, too, with studs in their eyebrows – some even had them in their tongues – and skirts up to the tops of their thighs. He knew what they got up to as well with the boys, not even bothering to hide away when they were doing it.

Phil liked working at The Grange, even if his father kept nagging him to get a proper job, as he put it. Unlike him, Fred was always nice to him, teaching him about the care of the various plants and always praising him if he did a good job and sometimes putting an arm round his shoulders when he was talking to him. The Traverses were all right, too, particularly Mrs Carlyle, Mrs Travers's widowed mother, who also lived in the house. She liked pottering in the garden and was always ready to have a word with him and made sure he was supplied with soft drinks in the summer and piping hot mugs of tea when winter came on. Unlike her mother, Mrs Travers didn't appear to have much interest in the garden and was hardly ever there, hurrying away in her car to attend some committee meeting or other, or carrying out fund raising activities for the Conservative party and being the loyal wife of her husband, who was a member of parliament. Phil hardly ever saw Mr Travers as he was either up in London, or working in his office in the town about three miles away. As to the three children, Matthew, who was seventeen and away most of the time at boarding school, seemed to think that he was lord of the manor and kept telling him to do things, such as putting away his tennis racket and the balls which he had left out and looking for missing golf balls which had escaped the netting where he had been practising his drives. Instead of having a chat, which Mr Travers always did when he met him, Matthew would, as just now, when Lizzie was showing him the fuchsia in her small pot, which she was growing for her grandmother's birthday in a few weeks' time, give him a curt nod and then look away as if a mere gardener's assistant didn't count for anything.

Lizzie, though, who was seven, was a nice and bright little girl. True, there were times when he wished she wouldn't chatter quite so much, but he did his best to answer the barrage of questions which she was always firing at him and she invariably thanked him when he helped her with the small plot that Fred had marked out for her in a corner of the kitchen garden. She was so proud of it and had never lost interest in looking after it.

As for Alex, the middle one who was sixteen, she was simply the most lovely girl he had ever seen and it wasn't only that; when they were hidden away in the copse near the pool, she showed him how to do things to her that made him blush every time he thought about them. On top of that were the risks she made him take, persuading him to do them at times when Fred or one of the family might so easily have caught them at it. She wasn't by any means always happy and excited, though; sometimes she would sob bitterly and be unable to explain what was wrong.

It got so that he could hardly think of anything else apart from her, particularly when he was lying in bed and unable to get off to sleep. She was just so pretty, with an amazing figure and didn't she know it? It was one thing when she was swimming in the pool near the tennis court, but why did her mother let her wander around the garden, wearing a skimpy top and the shortest of skirts, that had him wondering if she had anything on underneath? Perhaps, he thought, unlike the girl's grandmother, she didn't have the knack of being able to tell Lexie off without provoking floods of tears or screaming fits. Mrs Carlyle was such a calm and kind person and he often wished he had someone like her in whom he could confide and share some of his worries.

Behind the screen of trees at the bottom of the large lawn was a small pool, fed by a stream, which Mr Travers had arranged to have dug out, enlarged and shored up by massive boulders, which made it both large and big enough, not for swimming, but for floating on and plunging into when, like that day, it was hot and humid. Many was the time that he wished he wasn't just the gardener's boy and that he might have been able to use it himself more than that one time which he knew he would never forget.

As soon as he reached the edge of the copse, Phil saw, as

Fred had said, that quite a number of branches had come down and that there was a good deal of work to be done to collect them and no doubt saw them up for use in the house once they had dried out. Forty-five minutes later he was sweating uncomfortably, having moved a substantial amount of the fallen wood to the edge of the lawn and decided to go down to the pond beyond where he had been working to dip his hands and face into the water. He walked down the path and then came to an abrupt halt when he came in sight of it. A slim, naked figure was floating face down in the pond. For a fleeting moment, he thought that Lexie had heard him coming and that she was playing one of her tricks on him, but then he saw the blood staining the water. She was just out of his reach and he launched himself into the pond and pulled her out on to the bank.

He was later to wish that he had paid more attention to the first aid instruction they had all been given at school, but he did his best, trying not to be distracted by the sight of her battered face. He tried what he had remembered of the kiss of life despite the fact that her lower lip was cut and swollen, her nose obviously broken and one of her front teeth loose. He knew after only a minute or two that his efforts were going to be in vain and he stumbled back up the path, across the lawn and up the steps leading to the terrace at the back of the house and pounded on the door.

*

Commander Tyrrell shook his head irritably as he put down the receiver of his telephone. Why was it always his team that was picked when there were problems elsewhere? It was a complete waste of time even thinking about it, because he knew the answer already – they were just too damned good.

Fifteen minutes later, Mark Sinclair and Sarah Prescott came into his office at the Yard.

'Mark,' Tyrrell said, 'you no doubt remember DCS Watson.'

Sinclair certainly did. Detective Chief Superintendent Watson and even more his assistant, Alan Burgess, were the reasons why he had requested a transfer from Thames Valley to the Metropolitan Police, which he knew, as he glanced in Sarah's direction, had been the best decision he had made in his life.

'Yes, sir, only too well,' he replied.

'His unit is in bad trouble owing to the 'flu epidemic and he has a tricky case on his hands. I wasn't given any details, but it appears that the 16-year-old daughter of the local Tory MP, one Richard Travers, who evidently is also a landowner, was found dead, lying in the pool at the bottom of their garden having suffered various injuries to her face. It seems that an accident is out of the question and you will no doubt not be surprised to hear that the impetus behind the request for your help came from Henry Rawlings, the forensic pathologist, whom I gather you knew well when you were working down there, so perhaps it would be a good idea for you to see him first. I'd like you to go down there as soon as possible and I also think that Sarah should accompany you as I am led to believe that the murdered young girl was something of a handful.

'Now, I wasn't too happy with Watson's attitude on the phone. He's only got a few months left before his retirement; he's asking for a favour and yet he managed to give the impression that it was the other way round. I think he's frightened of getting involved in a high profile case that's bound to attract the interest of the media and he's never been good at thinking on his feet, particularly as he's got older and more crusty. The situation is further complicated in that the girl's grandfather, Sir Michael Travers, is a well known local figure, who happens to be chairman of the board of governors of the boarding school which the girl attended. Amongst other things, he is on the local police ethical standards committee. He very clearly carries a lot of clout down there.'

What Tyrrell didn't tell them was just how negative Watson had been when he had put forward Sinclair's name.

'Does it have to be him? I never could stand the supercilious bugger – he never fitted in here.'

'I should be very careful before you say anything further,' Tyrrell had said. 'I seem to recall that he pulled a few chestnuts out of the fire for you on your patch and he's one of the most able officers we have here who's shortly due for promo-

11

tion, which is why I am putting his name forward to you together with that of his partner. She is equally impressive, with particular experience of and skill in dealing with adolescent girls and it is also quite clear that the Traverses would appreciate the presence of a woman on the team. Now, let me have no more of this nonsense, otherwise you'll be looking elsewhere for help. Is that quite clear?'

Watson was shaken to the roots. He had no intention of apologizing, but knew he was on shaky ground, particularly as the father of the dead girl was a popular local MP, a toff himself and Sinclair would be just the man to impress him, not to mention Sir Michael, the grandfather. If either of them got any hint of what he had said to Tyrrell, it would very likely blight the respect he was anticipating following his retirement and his hopes of becoming a revered and influential figure in the local community.

'I'm sure that suitable accommodation will be found for you both,' Tyrrell said to the two detectives.

'Luckily there will be no need for that, sir,' Sinclair said. 'My widowed mother lives in that part of the world and I know she'll be only too pleased to put both of us up.'

'Good,' Tyrrell said, giving Sinclair a smile, knowing perfectly well that it wasn't only MPs who fiddled their expenses and that a lot of his colleagues took the view that as they were both underpaid and unappreciated, it was one way of redressing the balance. 'That means fewer expenses for me to have to justify, no bad thing with all the current fuss about that going on. Keep me posted, will you, and watch your step? Members of parliament need to be handled with kid gloves at the moment and a tragedy like this is bound to have hit the father hard, not least because the press are bound to latch on to it.'

Detective Chief Superintendent Watson was in a bad mood even before the appearance of Sinclair and the young woman with him. His deputy was still off sick with the 'flu, as were a number of the other staff, and they were run off their feet.

'You took your time getting here,' he said belligerently when they were shown into his office.

Sinclair looked at him for long enough before replying to bring an angry flush to his cheeks. It was just like Tyrrell, he thought, to send that snooty bastard, Sinclair, down, knowing perfectly well that he had never got on with him. He found the man's immaculate appearance and upper crust accent just as irritating as he had before. As for his partner, he had never approved of women in the force, let alone one who blushed when he stared at her, as if to say, 'what the hell's a dolly bird like you doing in a man's job?' The last thing he had wanted to do was to have to go cap in hand to London, particularly insulting when the suggestion had come from Sir Michael Travers, the grandfather of the dead girl and a man of great influence locally.

'You'll report to me here, both of you, at 8.30 every morning, to tell me what you are proposing to do and then after your first day, what you have achieved. Understood?'

'When I worked for you here, sir, you allowed me independence until I came across a situation that I was unable to deal with myself. Of course, we will be reporting to you when we need your help or there is some important development, but in view of the distances involved it is quite impractical to do so on the basis you suggest.'

'Oh, so you think that, do you?'

'Yes, sir, I do, and might I suggest that a call to Commander Tyrrell right now would be the best way to clarify the situation and to make sure that there are no further misunderstandings.'

It was just like the smooth bastard to put him on the back foot, Watson thought, knowing that Tyrrell had already made clear where his support lay and that Sir Michael Travers would have plenty to say about it, too, if he started putting objections forward.

'Very well, but I insist on being kept informed of any progress you make and you'd better get a move on. Is that quite understood?'

'Neither my colleague nor I have any problem with that. We will be meeting Dr Rawlings this afternoon.'

'To my shame,' Sarah said, on their way to the forensic pathologist, 'I thought you were exaggerating when you told me about Watson, but you weren't; in fact it was a masterly understatement.'

Sinclair laughed. 'I reckon I've got his number now and, what's more, he knows it.'

Another surprise, which he most certainly hadn't been anticipating, was the reaction of Miss Ryle, the forensic pathologist's secretary, to their arrival at his office.

The woman whom he had remembered as being both thin and acerbic, had now obviously put on a little weight, and greeted them both with a warm smile and said: 'Good to see you again, sir.'

'And you, Miss Ryle. May I introduce my partner, Inspector Sarah Prescott?'

The woman inclined her head. 'Pleased to meet you, ma'am.'

'Managed to avoid the dreaded 'flu, have you, Miss Ryle?' Sinclair asked.

'Yes, thank goodness. You should hear what Dr Rawlings has to say about people taking two weeks off for what he terms "a godsend for the work-shy".'

'So the bug hasn't attacked him yet, then?'

'I don't think it would dare to do so, sir.'

Sinclair raised his eyebrows slightly. 'That I can well believe.'

'I'll tell Dr Rawlings that you're here; he was saying only this morning how much he was looking forward to meeting you both.'

To Sinclair's surprise, the forensic pathologist got up from his chair and shook him vigorously by the hand when they were shown in.

'Welcome, my dear fellow. Very good to see you again and to make your acquaintance, my dear,' he said. 'My old friend and some time chess adversary, Eric Tredgold, was telling me about the two of you only the other day when we met at a conference. You're quite the rising stars of the Met, I was led to believe.'

'I wouldn't say that exactly,' Sinclair replied with a smile, 'but it certainly has been a pleasure working with Roger Tyrrell.'

'Yes. I've heard about him from Tredgold. Good man, is he?'

'First rate.'

'Right. Enough of this luvvie stuff, an expression that Miss Ryle assures me is quite démodé and I, for one, will be glad to see the back of it if that really is the case. Now, we have an intriguing case here with, I gather, all sorts of social and political overtones, but, as a mere pathologist, the finer points of that haven't come my way yet. However, the bare bones are as follows: the gardener's boy who works on the estate of one of our local MPs, one Richard Travers, was sent down to clear the branches, which had been brought down from a copse at the bottom of the substantial garden in a thunderstorm the night before. In a clearing at the back of that wood, there is quite a small pond, which is fed by a stream and which Travers had enlarged by having it dug out and some large boulders introduced round the perimeter. It is not big enough for swimming and floating and paddling are about all that are possible. It is mainly used for sitting on one of the flat rocks bordering it and dangling one's feet in the water. There is also a formal swimming pool with a diving board on the other side of the garden.' Rawlings looked at Sinclair across the desk. 'May I trouble you to pull the curtains across?'

When the detective complied, he switched on the projector, inserted a slide and turned off the anglepoise light on his desk.

'The gardener's boy found the girl about here, lying face down in the water,' he said, indicating the centre of the pool with his pointer. 'As soon as he saw her, the young fellow waded in, pulled her up on to the grassy area between it and the copse and tried an approximation of the artificial respiration he had been shown in life saving classes at school, rather bravely, in my opinion, as her face was quite badly damaged. He continued his efforts for several minutes and when it was obvious that the girl was dead, he ran up the lawn and hammered on the door on the terrace. The girl's mother, Mrs Travers, was out, but her grand-mother, one Mrs Carlyle, who also lives in the house, when she had heard what the boy had to say, didn't waste time by going down to the pond herself, immediately ringing for an ambulance. Finding the girl dead, the crew alerted the police and I was called in very soon afterwards.

'The next slide shows the girl lying on her back, completely naked, on the grass in the clearing I mentioned,

17

where the boy left her when he dashed up to the house and as the ambulance people found her. I'll show you a selection of the pictures taken there. Taking into account the findings on the boulder above the pool, the most likely scenario is that she had been lying there on her front on her towel, reading a paperback, both of which are shown on the next slide. Presumably she heard something behind her, because there were no blood stains on her towel and the evidence points to her having been standing facing in the opposite direction when she was hit on the left side of her jaw, hard enough to have fractured it and to have loosened some teeth. It seems that she then fell to her right, bruising her right hip and elbow, which you can see in the next two slides. She appears not to have made any attempt to put out either her hand or arm to ward off the blow and was almost certainly unconscious when she hit the water. There is no doubt at all that the cause of death was drowning, water being present in her air passages.

'I found no other abnormality. She was well developed for her stated age of sixteen and she had been sexually active in the past, but nothing to suggest rape of either sort or of normal intercourse a short time before her death.'

'Have you any idea what might have caused the injury to her face?' Sinclair asked.

'Could have been a flat stone, or just possibly a fist.'

'If it had been the latter, would the fist have been damaged as well.'

'Most probably, if it had belonged to a sedentary worker, but not necessarily if it had been a manual labourer.'

'But definitely a male rather than female.'

'Without doubt. As to another weapon, an intensive search was made for one, such as a blood-stained stone, but none was found.'

'Do you know roughly what time she fell into the water, sir?' Sarah, asked.

Rawlings gave her one of his vulpine grins. 'No need for the formalities, young lady. It's true that I prefer "sir" to "mate" or "old cock", but if some variety of formal address should strike you as being necessary, then Dr Rawlings would suffice. I digress and in answer to your question, it was a few seconds after 9.41.'

'Which presumably means that she was wearing a watch at the time that had stopped after its immersion in the water.'

Rawlings laughed. 'No flies on you, my dear. Yes, she was and it did.'

'What about the family?' Sinclair asked.

'Travers, the girl's father, is the local Conservative MP and although I've never met him, I do know his father, Sir Michael, quite well – we are members of the same golf club, not that either of us is in the same league as you, my dear Sinclair. Now, the reason for my telling you that is not to boast about my social connections, but to explain why you were approached through Tyrrell. You see, another member of the golf club is Sir Geoffrey Belling.'

Sinclair nodded. 'Now I'm beginning to understand.'

Rawlings grinned at him. 'I thought you might. You see, my dear,' he said turning towards Sarah Prescott, 'your partner was instrumental in uncovering the murderer of the daughter of Belling's chauffeur a few years back and Sir Geoffrey was mightily impressed, so much so that when he heard about the untimely death of Travers's granddaughter, he suggested to him that you should be the man to be called in, rather than that bull in a china shop, Watson, and his even more unpleasant sidekick, Burgess. The 'flu epidemic providentially dealt with the latter and, not surprisingly, Watson being close to retirement, had no wish to antagonize Travers, nor his son, so he agreed....

'Now, I've never met the girl's father, Richard Travers, and the person you need is my wife, Helen, who knows him quite well. We live in a small village only a mile or two from the town and dare I say it, she was a great admirer of Margaret Thatcher and is heavily into fund raising for the cause and the town's activities as well. I'm sure she would be glad to give you some information about him. Why not give her a ring late this evening after I've had a chance to warn her of the impending inquisition?

'I see your look of astonishment at my mellow attitude, my dear fellow,' Rawlings said, glancing sideways at Sinclair. 'It surprises Miss Ryle and I'm even surprised by it myself; perhaps it's due to the prospect of retirement in the not too distant future or even the effect of advancing years.'

Sinclair decided to let that one pass. 'Do you have a note of the GP's address and phone number, by any chance? We'll obviously have to make our number with the parents first, but the GP will also have to be an early port of call.'

'Good idea.'

Rawlings pressed the buzzer on his desk and the secretary appeared so quickly that if Sinclair hadn't known her so well, he might have suspected that she had been trying to listen in to their conversation.

'Ah, Miss Ryle, attentive as ever, I see. First things first, some refreshment to start with, if you please, and then the name and telephone number of the Travers's GP.'

To the two detectives' amazement, the woman nodded and within a minute or two returned with a trolley on which was a plate of buttered scones with generous dollops of jam on them as well as a large cafetière of coffee and a small, but very elegant Royal Doulton jug with cream in it.

Rawlings waited until the woman had departed and then let out a loud guffaw. 'I see by your facial expression that you are no doubt wondering, my dear Sinclair, what has happened to the acerbic dragon, who was always nagging me about my weight and cholesterol. Why the appearance of largesse, sweet reason and benignity all of a sudden? Well you might ask. Are you thinking that romance might have entered her life? No? Of course you bloody well aren't. If you ask me, there is only one credible explanation and that is the departure from this life of her tyrannical old mother. I only met her the once and I can tell you that one look from her was enough to curdle the milk, even if it was in the fridge.'

At that moment, there was a knock on the door and the secretary came in again and handed a piece of paper to the pathologist.

'The GP is a Dr Hazel Mead and I've written her address and phone number down for you, sir. She's a member of the group practice that occupies the new health centre in the town, which, as it happens, was opened by Mr Travers about three years ago. She is not married. I have also taken the liberty of adding the same information about the Conservative Party office as I understand that Mr Travers is often there during the parliamentary recess. I gather that he holds a surgery in the town when he is here on Tuesday afternoons. Might I suggest that I ring his secretary for an appointment, perhaps after that has finished?'

'Miss Ryle! Divining our needs before being asked! Such perspicacity is indeed to be wondered at.' He glanced at the two detectives. 'That suit you both?'

'Admirably,' Sinclair replied. 'We are staying with my mother not that far away and it will give us a chance to unpack and settle in there.'

Sinclair had the unlikely thought that Miss Ryle might have believed that a miracle had happened and that Rawlings had mellowed beyond belief. However, the slight raising of the eyebrows as she looked in the detective's direction as they left, made it quite clear that she hadn't been taken in for a moment.

'They're like a comedy duo, those two; have they always been like that?' Sarah asked as they drove to Mrs Sinclair's house some ten miles from the country town, where Richard Travers held his surgeries.

'Yes, certainly all the time I worked in his area of operations, is the short answer to that, but the style has altered. He is a great deal more mellow than I remember and she certainly appears much more cheerful. Perhaps he really is getting demob happy.'

There was a large free car park in the centre of the town, with a supermarket, bakery and a row of small shops at one end of it, while behind it, the tower of the church was visible through some trees and along the road was a row of nineteenth-century terrace houses. In a number of them, the ground floors had been converted into accommodation for an estate agent, a solicitor's office, a ladies' hairdresser and a coffee shop. In one of them was the Conservative Party office and when they rang the bell late that afternoon, it was answered by a smartly dressed young woman, who looked to be in her middle twenties.

'My name is Maria Coleman and I'm Mr Travers's secretary,' she said with a smile. 'And you must be the detective inspectors from London.'

'That's right,' Sarah said, shaking the young woman's

hand, 'I'm Sarah Prescott and this is my colleague, Mark Sinclair.'

'Perhaps you'd like to wait in here. Mr Travers is on the telephone at the moment, but I'm sure he won't be long.'

Richard Travers proved to be a tall, slim, good-looking man whom, Sinclair thought, must be well into his forties, but he didn't look it, having thick black hair without a hint of grey in it and an athletic figure.

'I'm very pleased to see you both,' he said. 'I'm sure you must be well aware that politicians are not exactly the flavour of the moment at present and my wife and I are naturally very anxious that this very sad affair should be cleared up as soon as possible.'

'We hope to be able to see your wife first thing tomorrow morning and wondered if that would be convenient for her. Perhaps you would kindly give her a ring to confirm it?'

'Of course, I'll do so right away. I have to be up in London first thing, so won't be able to join you then, but I'm in no hurry this afternoon.'

After the man had confirmed that his wife would expect them soon after nine the following morning, Travers smiled at them across the desk and said: 'Now, what is it that you'd like to discuss with me?'

'First we would very much like to hear your view of your daughter, Alex,' Sinclair said.

The man nodded. 'My mother-in-law, who has lived with us since her husband died some ten years ago, would be the best person to put you fully into the picture regarding Alex, because she was the one who spent the most time with her, my wife being occupied at first with a new baby and then latterly working with a women's organization in Oxford. I should perhaps explain first how we came to adopt Alex. To put it briefly, we already had a son, Matthew, who is now just eighteen, and when five years had gone by after he was born and we failed to achieve another child, we made the decision to adopt Alex, which we did through a Church of England organization. We were anxious that there shouldn't be too big a gap between Matthew and the new child and it so happened that we were able to welcome Alex, who was two and a bit at that time, just over two years younger than him. Some six years later, Maddy became pregnant again, despite the gloomy prognosis of the obstetricians, and our younger daughter, Elizabeth was born then.

'I'd rather leave Madeleine and, in particular, my mother-in-law, to describe the problems we had with Alex over the years, but as I was heavily involved with the events that occurred during our family holiday in Corfu last Easter, I'd better put you into the picture with regard to that. At that time, Alex was physically an extremely attractive young lady, being very pretty and looking more than her age. We had already had difficulties with her as she had always been very emotional, alternating between being happy and vivacious and in the depths of despair.

25

Anyway, all of us, except my mother-in-law, went on holiday to Corfu during the Easter break and Alex spent a lot of her time swimming in the sea or in the hotel pool. She had saved some of her pocket money and, unbeknown to us, bought a highly unsuitable bikini while out there, but as a lot of the other young girls in the hotel were wearing similar ones, we decided not to make an issue over it. Perhaps, though, we ought to have noticed that the son of the proprietor of the hotel, who was not much older than Alex, was taking a good deal more than a casual interest in her, but to start with we had no idea just how much more.

'Anyway, one afternoon, without asking our permission and while Madeleine was having a siesta and I was reading a book on the balcony of our room facing the sea, I saw him taking her for a row. If they had remained in sight in the bay, I would, of course not have had any worries, but when they disappeared round the headland, I decided to take a walk along the cliff up there to see what they were up to. It took me a good half hour to get a view of the secluded cove below and my worst fears were realized when I saw them making love down on the small beach there.

'I should tell you that my family are staunch members of the Church of England and initially there was a bit of a problem with them when I started to go out with Madeleine, whose parents were, how shall I put it, distinctly lacking in interest in any form of religion.

Fortunately, Madeleine became an enthusiastic member of our church and we are both practising Christians ourselves. Needless to say, our daughter having premarital sex, let alone at her age, was something we couldn't possibly tolerate and, in my position as an MP, I'm sure you understand what a field day the press would have had if what Alex had been up to were to become common knowledge.

'I have already said that we have had our difficulties with Alex, but that is a major understatement; she was something of a nightmare right from the time we adopted her, being very up and down emotionally. Anyway, after a long discussion with my wife, we decided that I should take the girl back to England from Corfu straight away, where we knew that my highly competent mother-in-law would the best person to handle her.'

'And that's what you did?'

'Yes and I suppose one might say that it didn't work out too badly. There were floods of tears from Alex, a promise that she wouldn't see the boy, nor do anything like that again, but we weren't prepared to take the risk of her continuing to stay at the hotel. I did see the boy myself and put the fear of God into him, telling him that he was lucky that I wasn't going to tell his father, who was known for his temper and would almost certainly have beaten the daylights out of him had he known what had happened and I decided to leave it at that.

'I did consider going back to Corfu myself after I had brought Alex back here, but decided that it wouldn't be fair to leave my mother-in-law literally holding the baby, so to speak. Both of us thought that the return to England was punishment enough and we tried to give Alex a good time for the rest of the holiday, taking her to a game park, to the local swimming pool – ours is unheated and hadn't been filled at that time – and to a film. I also practised tennis with her. In addition to all that, I arranged for her to see our very sympathetic, young female GP. I told her what had happened and asked her to have a chat to Lexie about sex, as neither Madeleine nor I felt up to it, particularly as I had been told that her boarding school had handled that side of things with special talks.'

'And it worked out all right?'

'It seemed to. Alex went back to school and during the present holidays, she seemed to have calmed down a bit.'

'Did your son know what had happened?'

'Matthew is also a bit of a worry to us, but in the opposite direction. He takes after my mother, who died last year. Unlike my father, who is a live wire, always cheerful and outgoing, she took life very seriously and, to be honest, was never a bundle of fun. Matthew is very much tarred with the same brush, being rather rigid and obsessional and has already been talking about being ordained when he finishes school. My father and I are concerned about that as we both consider that he is far too young, particularly in the emotional sense, to make a decision like that. It may be rather a harsh thing to say, but Matthew seems to me to be joyless, lacking a sense of humour and even, dare I say it, middle-aged in outlook. Quite deliberately, we have never spoken to Matthew about our worries and problems with Alex, but he's no fool and must have picked up something about them as it's quite obvious that since that event in Corfu he clearly wanted to have as little to do with her as possible. His interests are religion, academic work and sport, in that order and he obviously goes down very well at his rather rigid boarding school. My father and I went to the same place ourselves and we both rebelled against a lot of what we both considered petty rules that were in place then and the overtly pious attitude of many of the masters. I wasn't at all keen on Matthew following me there, but my mother, who was obsessed, there is no other word for it, with religion, made a lot of fuss about it and I gave in, knowing that Matthew was made for a place like that and it didn't seem worth while having a major row with her about it. I am concerned about him, though, in other ways; he seems old before his time and, dare I say it, pompous, but he obviously fits in perfectly well at that particular school.'

'How did Matthew get on with Alex before the events in Corfu?'

'The short answer to that is that he didn't. He thought that she was frivolous, without a thought in her head apart from clothes and constantly making an exhibition of herself. With hindsight, I believe that her arrival when he was seven put his nose out of joint and he resented her right from the beginning and the attention we gave her. Later on, I think he was scared of her.'

'Why scared?'

'Because of her overt sexuality and physical attractiveness. Matthew finds the very idea, let alone the practice of sex, abhorrent and I suspect that he has been having too many talks with one of the rigid, puritanical masters at his school. There is no doubt, too, that the situation got a lot worse after Alex reached puberty. As for our youngest child, Lizzie, she is a delight, a free spirit and happy soul. Even Matthew unbends a bit with her and, to my astonishment, I saw him in Corfu helping her to build a sandcastle. I say helping, but that isn't true; he took over and although it was most impressive, it was hardly Lizzie's work, although she didn't seem to mind, obviously enjoying fetching buckets of sea water for him.'

'What about Alex's school?' Sarah asked.

'I didn't really want her to go to boarding school, but it was obvious that she was proving altogether too much of a handful for Maddy and if anything it was getting worse the older she got. A bonus of the school to which we did send her was the fact that my father is chairman of the board of governors and he takes an active interest in it. He lives not all that far away from it and on some Sundays used to take Alex and her friend out to lunch. I also felt that we could hardly expect my mother-in-law, Anne Carlyle, who has lived with us since the death of her husband seven or eight years ago, to manage a difficult adolescent during term time as well as the holidays. I have to say, though, that she was brilliant with Alex and was the one person who was able to calm her down and even tell her off without provoking violent emotions of one sort or another.'

'So your mother-in-law had known Alex ever since she was about eight?'

'No, longer than that, because when her husband was alive, she often used to have her round to her house after school, which was only about twenty minutes' drive away.'

'Do you know anything about Alex's natural parents?'

'Not a thing. I understand that she was left on the doorstep of an Anglican church when she was only a week or two old and later on went to an orphanage, run by a Church of England foundation, which is where she still was when we adopted her.'

'Did she have any special friends of either sex near here?'

'No, but she did have one at her boarding school, a girl by the name of Rosie Maxwell, who came to stay with us here a couple of times and Lexie also had a short holiday at her house near Reading. I have to say that I didn't take to the girl all that much – she hardly said a word to any of us all the time she was here – but the two of them were as thick as thieves. Unfortunately, they were involved in some silly prank at their school about six months ago – they were fooling about in one of the showers together. To make matters worse, they were discovered by one of the student teachers, a distinctly intense young woman, who had been seconded to the school for a term's work experience. Instead of reporting the matter to her superior, the housemistress, she went straight to the headmistress, who, to be honest, has a distinctly rigid personality and a pathological fear of the press getting on to that sort of thing. Luckily, my father, as chairman of the board of governors, became involved and although he's a very relaxed and laid back person, he can be pretty imposing when he chooses. I gather that he made it very clear that disciplinary action of that sort would be too extreme and would almost certainly lead to just the sort of publicity that Miss Elliott was fearing. Once my father had heard the evidence, which he considered to be unreliable, he made it quite clear that in his view expulsion was inappropriate in a case such as that and totally disproportionate to the offence, there being not a shred of evidence of any sexual impropriety having taken place, which the young student had assumed.

'As a result, both girls received a serious telling off, had some privileges withdrawn for the rest of that term and that was the end of it.'

'And how did the two girls react to that?'

'It all happened last winter term. We heard nothing further about it and Madeleine and I decided that the incident was best left to be handled by the school.'

'How did you manage Alex at home as far as discipline was concerned?'

'I have to say that Madeleine found her extremely difficult to handle and gave her a hand spanking a few times and once even hit her with the back of a clothes brush. I only knew about that because I saw the bruises when Alex was wearing her bikini and the bottom part had ridden up a bit and when I asked her how it had happened, she told me. I don't need to tell you that that level of punishment is both unacceptable and illegal nowadays and I tackled Madeleine about it.'

'When was that?'

'About eighteen months ago.'

'How did your wife react to that?

'She was absolutely furious and things have not been quite the same between us ever since. She said that it was all very well for me to talk, when I had so little to do with Lexie's upbringing and didn't seem to realize how difficult the girl was, and that corporal punishment had been the only way of dealing with her. Anyway, that problem was resolved when my mother-in-law became even more involved with Alex. She took the same stance about that sort of discipline as me. She was much more tactful, though, with Maddy than I had been, and managed to get the message across without creating too much fuss and with a promise that it wouldn't happen again.'

'There seems to be no doubt that Alex was sunbathing down by the pool in the nude on the morning that she died. Did you or your wife know that she was in the habit of doing that?'

'I don't know about Maddy, but I certainly didn't, not that I would have been unduly worried had I done so. Girls, or boys for that matter, at boarding schools, aren't as bothered by nudity as their counterparts at day schools, particularly those in the state system. As for Madeleine, I'm quite certain that she would have disapproved strongly. I don't want to give the wrong impression, just let me say that she has strong views about proprieties and Alex's behaviour in some respects both concerned and upset her. As far as I know, she still doesn't know that Alex was found naked and Mrs Carlyle, who handled the situation admirably, after discussing it with me, decided not to tell her and I have to say that I believe she did the right thing. A further point, selfish if you like, is that were the tabloids to get hold of this, it doesn't require much imagination to realize what a field day they would make of it, and I still worry about it, as sooner or later it's almost certain to come out, but "sufficient until the day is the evil thereof".'

'Have you any idea, or even a theory about who might have been responsible for the whole dreadful affair?'

'Believe me, Madeleine, her mother, and I have gone over it ad nauseam and the one half sensible idea we had was that some vagrant might have climbed over the wall around the estate the previous evening, possibly looking for shelter from the thunderstorm and dossed down in the wood, went to sleep and when he woke, found Alex sunbathing and tried to rape her. Perhaps, we thought, she had tried to defend herself and that was when she was assaulted and thrown into the water. I have already been told that there is no evidence that Alex was in fact raped. I might say I have not even hinted at such a possibility to Madeleine, or anyone else in the family. It would undoubtedly have upset them, particularly her, too much.'

'What staff do you have at home?'

'There is the housekeeper, Mrs Weston and the cook, Mrs Parsmore, both of whom live in. They each have a bedroom on the third floor and share a sitting room down by the kitchen. There is also a cleaner from the village, who comes in every day except at weekends and then there is the gardener and a boy, both of whom live nearby. Fred Palmer was the gardener here when we bought the place ten years ago and we agreed to keep him on. I have never regretted it. He may be getting on a bit and be somewhat morose, but he works hard and gets on well with my mother-in-law, who is very knowledgeable about flowers. His assistant, one Phil Carter, joined him a year ago when he finished school. He must be about seventeen now, a bit younger than Matthew.'

35

'What's he like?'

'A very nice, rather shy boy. He's been particularly good with Lizzie, helping her with a little plot that he marked out for her in the kitchen garden. Maddy tells me that Fred has very much taken Phil under his wing and my mother-in-law also gets on well with him, as she does with everyone else.'

'I'm sure you understand that we are going to have to go over the site of this tragedy with the head of the scene-of-crime officers. We have an appointment with him tomorrow afternoon. You probably know that his team has already inspected the grounds and Alex's room carefully and we would like to talk to everyone in the house, with the possible exception of Lizzie, and also visit Alex's school,' Sinclair said.

'Yes, of course and I've already warned Maddy that that was likely to happen. I also had a word with her about Lizzie. She is nearly eight now and we have no objection to one of you, I would suggest Inspector Prescott, if I may, having a brief word with her. She is not the sort of child to be upset by that if handled gently. I have also taken the liberty of telling everyone in the house that they are on no account to speak to the press. That does remain a worry, though; they have deep pockets and they're bound to start ferreting around at the local pubs. I have, of course, been in touch with the party leader. He is very good with the media and has already been most supportive to me.'

*

'What did you make of him?' Sinclair asked when they were back in the car.

'I've not met any politicians before, other than very casually, but I've seen a great many on TV, either being interviewed, or appearing on various chat shows and inevitably there is a broad spectrum, from the charming and articulate to the aggressive and rude. Travers obviously comes from the former group, but I was surprised how forthcoming he was to us. And did I detect that there appears to be some friction between him and his wife? I also wonder what goes on behind the facade of good manners and like so many of his colleagues, he's obviously good at thinking on his feet, but is he really as detached as he appears to be? After all, his daughter, admittedly adopted and a major handful, has been brutally murdered only a short time ago and here he is urbane and seemingly not unduly depressed by what has happened and totally in control of himself.'

'I agree and what about that secretary of his? Did you get the same impression as I did, that there is something going on between them?'

Sarah nodded. 'I most certainly did. Did you notice what happened when we were shown to the door on our way out?'

'No, I can't say that I did.'

'The young woman was standing to one side and just

behind him and I saw her pick a bit of fluff off the shoulder of his jacket, hardly the sort of intimate gesture that most secretaries go in for.'

'Certainly not Miss Ryle, for one.' Sinclair grinned at her as she cuffed him on the shoulder. 'That's a good point, which I failed to pick up.'

TWO

AFTER THEY HAD entered through the gates of the
Travers's property in the car, the house came into view
almost immediately. It looked to Sinclair as if it had originally been an eighteenth-century manor house, but quite
clearly it had been enlarged with later additions. It was
built of mellow Cotswold stone and was in some three acres
of ground, bordered by a stone wall with mature trees at the
base of the large lawn at the back. To one side was a
substantial kitchen garden and beyond it there was a hard
tennis court and a swimming pool.

'I imagine that the stream and pool are at the bottom of
the lawn and beyond those trees.' Sarah said.

'It certainly seems like it.'

Mrs Travers, who answered the front doorbell herself,
looked to be in her early forties. From their research, they
knew that she had been a successful three day event rider in
her younger days and it appeared as if she had kept up riding
in some shape or form as she was both trim and with well
marked definition in the muscles of her bare arms.

'Why don't we go into the drawing room?' she said when the introductions had been made and Sarah told her that they had already had a chat with her husband.

'Yes,' she said, 'he gave me a ring just after you left him.'

Like her husband, with her daughter's death only having occurred a few days earlier, she was remarkably composed, Sarah thought, and she hardly hesitated when asked to give them an impression of the girl that Alex had been.

'I think it would be helpful were I to explain how we came to adopt Alex when she was three years old, give you an idea of what sort of girl she was and put her in context with our other two children.

'Our first child, Matthew, who is just eighteen, is just the sort of young man my husband and I predicted he would become when he was quite small. Very driven and ambitious, he is a hard worker, both at his school studies and at sport, which is a major interest of his. He has a very even temperament, some would say unemotional, but that's not true; he has extremely strong religious beliefs and a very clear idea of what is right and what is wrong. I must say that I have often wondered what the other boys at his public school make of him. I know that he has had ideas about taking holy orders, not a complete surprise as one of his uncles is a Church of England bishop, but my husband and I feel he is too young to make a final decision about that. His housemaster at his boarding school agrees and although he is convinced that Matthew is entirely sincere

40

and even hinted that he might have a true vocation, he believes that further study and the chance to mature fully would be the best way forwards. No doubt some of his contemporaries find him pious in the extreme and rather dull from their point of view. You see, he has no interest whatever in alcohol, drugs or loud music and he doesn't have a girlfriend. Like my husband before him, he goes to the same single sex boarding school and several of our friends have questioned our decision over that, something to which we both take exception as Matthew is obviously quite content with his life and sincere in his beliefs. A social life is not something that interests him at all at present and I do worry about that at times, but as my husband says, adolescence is a difficult time for a lot of young people, particularly with all the temptations of sex and drugs, and we should give thanks that we have no worries with him in either of those directions.

'Before I come to Alex, perhaps I should explain about Lizzie. You see, we had been trying for another child for a good six years after Matthew was born without any luck and that's when we decided to go in for the adoption of a girl. We didn't want there to be too big a gap between them and that was why we went for a child aged three or there-abouts. You may imagine our joy when five years after she came to us I became pregnant with Lizzie, something I was told is not that rare an occurrence after an adoption. Afterwards nothing else has happened in that direction and although we had always wanted a big family, to be blessed with three was more than we had expected. Lizzie is now seven and is a very happy, sociable child. She is neither as intense nor as clever as Matthew, but she has an even and uncomplicated temperament and is very popular at her primary school. The others want to sit next to her in class and at meals and to be her friend. She is a very physical child, who loves running about, swimming and going on the swing and the trampoline. She's certainly no saint, in fact a bit of a pickle and as bright as a button, as my mother would say, and she's very good for me and my husband as we undoubtedly tend to take life more than a bit too seriously. My guess would be that she will sail through it untroubled and cheerful.

'My husband and I, like his parents, are committed Christians and after I failed to conceive for several years after Matthew's birth despite the best medical advice, we went to a Church of England adoption society when he was five and Alex was the result. She was roughly two and a half when she came to us and straight away it was obvious that she had an entirely different personality from the rest of us. Unlike Matthew, our son, who is very serious-minded and unemotional, rather like my late mother-in-law, Alex was quite different. With her it was a roller coaster ride. She could be sweet and thoughtful, but those occasions became rarer as she got older. Even as a young child, she used to have terrible temper tantrums, such that she would throw china onto the floor, screaming and kicking when anybody tried to restrain her. At others she would cry uncontrollably, sometimes for up to half an hour without stopping. I remember one occasion when she did so after seeing a dead bird lying on this terrace over there.

'She could also be embarrassingly physical, throwing herself at visitors she didn't know well, hugging them and snuggling up to them when sitting beside them on the sofa. I remember vividly the occasion she did so with one of my husband's constituency workers, a starchy elderly woman, who was always complaining about something or other. It was really embarrassing to me before I suddenly saw that the woman was almost in tears and I realized that quite possibly no one had done that to her before or at least for years. On another occasion, when she was older, I found Alex standing in her bedroom in her nightie looking out of the window with tears streaming down her cheeks. I asked her what was wrong and she replied: "It's the moon, it's just so beautiful".'

'Did you have any problems with sex once she reached adolescence? Sarah asked.

'I was coming to that. By the time she was thirteen we had been finding it increasingly difficult to deal with her behaviour, and we sent her to a boarding school with a strong Christian tradition. For a time she seemed to get on reasonably well there, but last summer term, I was asked to go up to see the headmistress, Miss Elliott. She said that

Alex and another girl had been found by a student teacher taking a shower together. Unfortunately, that young woman, instead of going to the proper authority, her housemistress, went straight to the Head and told her that the two of them had been behaving inappropriately. It was quite obvious that Miss Elliott didn't approve of the young woman having bypassed the housemistress and was concerned that the matter might get out of hand and even leaked to the press. Anyway, my father-in-law, who is chairman of the board of governors and a very calm person and extremely good with people, got to hear about it and dealt with the situation. Both girls had the privileges that they were allowed withdrawn for the rest of the term and the headmistress made it clear that if there was a recurrence of any behaviour like that, both Alex and the other girl would have to leave the school. Both my husband and I had a meeting with the headmistress; she told us about the steps she had taken and we promised to tackle Alex ourselves as well.'

'And presumably you did?'

'Yes. As I've already said, Alex had always been a very tactile child and she told me that she and the other girl had just been fooling about. I asked her in what way and she said that they had just been tickling each other and had been making rather a lot of noise. Perhaps I should have questioned her more closely, but partly because, I have to admit, I couldn't face it and partly because if she was telling me the truth I didn't want to stir things up too much, I didn't. My husband, though, who always had the knack of handling Alex's uncertain behaviour better than me, agreed to deal with the problem more formally.'

'Do you know what he said to her?'

'Not in detail, but he told me that he had pointed out to her that she had been very stupid and explained that these days school teachers had a very difficult job to do and that discipline was very hard to maintain when direct physical punishment of children, boys as well as girls, was against the law. He finished by telling her that there was on no account to be any further behaviour of that sort.

'He clearly thought that just tickling another girl, even if it was in the shower, should hardly have been dealt with by the threat of expulsion, but decided that it would be counterproductive to press her too hard.'

'Had there been any further trouble of that nature since?'

'Not at school, but Fred, the gardener, who is a bit of a grouch in my opinion – don't tell my mother I said so because she won't have a word said against him – complained to me a few weeks ago that Alex was always asking his assistant, Phil, to do little jobs for her and told me that she had come up to the young man wearing only her bikini to ask him to clear some nettles which were over-hanging the path down to the pool.'

'Did you do anything about that?'

'Yes, I told Alex that she shouldn't interrupt Phil's work,

and if something like that needed to be done, she should tell me or my mother and we would deal with it directly with the gardening staff. I wish I had taken it more seriously because last Easter there was an incident with the son of the owner of the hotel we were staying at in Corfu, which I understand my husband has already discussed with you. He managed to handle it without letting the father of the boy know what had happened. We were also well aware that the press in England would have a field day over it if they discovered that Alex, at that time, at fifteen still under age, had been having sex on the beach. We both agreed that the most sensible solution would be for Richard to take her back to England and we made up a story that she had been getting bad stomach pains and we were concerned about the possibility of appendicitis. I knew that my mother, who has always been very good with Alex, much better than me, would be at home, which was a great comfort to me.

'My husband can be pretty imposing if he wants to and he told the boy that if he so much as said a word to anyone or even boasted about what the two of them had been doing on the beach, he would find out and the chances were that he would end up in prison on top of what his father might do to him. He must have convinced him, because I stayed on with Matthew and Lizzie for the rest of the holiday and there was not the slightest hint that our story hadn't been accepted and the boy in question kept well out of the way. It all seemed to have worked out well and I deliberately didn't bring the matter up with Alex when we got back as both my husband and my mother assured me that together they had tackled her just the once and the result was floods of tears. She told them that she had got carried away and promised that she wouldn't do anything like that ever again and it soon became obvious that she wasn't pregnant, which would have been the ultimate disaster, as the family as a whole, for various moral and religious reasons, would not have countenanced a termination. The press would also no doubt have found out and the resulting publicity would have been a serious matter as far as my husband's career was concerned.'

'Did you leave it at that as far as Alex was concerned?'

'To be honest, I felt completely out of my depth and anyway, my husband had already arranged for Alex to have a consultation with our GP, a young married woman, before I returned from Greece with the others. I didn't press Alex or my husband into telling me what had been said, but Alex appeared to have settled down reasonably well and I found her a job helping out at one of the local old peoples' homes until school started the following week. When she came back for the present holiday, she seemed rather quieter and I thought that at last she was really settling down and then this had to happen.'

For this first time since the two detectives had met her, the woman showed some emotion and dabbed her eyes with her handkerchief.

'It's very upsetting to us that the local police have sealed Alex's bedroom,' Mrs Travers said, her voice breaking slightly. 'Will I be allowed to go in there soon?'

'I assure you that you will be able to do so within the next day or two, but we will have to be shown round it ourselves first – we have an appointment with one of the experts from the local force later this afternoon and we'll also be going down to the wood. Have you any idea at all who might have wanted to harm your daughter?'

'Believe me, my husband and I have thought of almost nothing else since it happened. As you may have already seen, there is a stone wall all around the perimeter of the property, but someone could have got in easily enough, and before you ask, we are not the sort of people to make enemies. Both of us and my mother have done a lot for the local community and no one could have pointed the finger at Richard over MPs' expenses. He has never claimed other than the barest minimum, mainly concerned with his office in the town. Lexie didn't have any real friends in the village – her special ones were at school and one of them has been to stay here a couple of times.'

'Who was here at the time of your daughter's tragic death?' Sinclair asked.

'Well, as far as the grounds were concerned, I understand that Fred, the gardener, was having a cup of tea with Mrs Parsmore, our cook, while waiting for Phil, his assistant, who was at the dentist. It was he who found her, when, later on, after he had been clearing the branches from the trees near the pond, which had come down in the thunderstorm the previous night, he went down there to dip his face in the water, because he had got so hot, and that's when he found Lexie. My mother was helping Lizzie with her knitting in the drawing room and I had already driven off towards Oxford, where I was going to the book club I attend regularly with a group of my women friends.'

'Do you remember what time you left?'

'I'm not sure. You see, things were a bit fraught that morning. Matthew wasn't feeling well at breakfast and the other two were playing up a bit. I put it down to the disturbed night we'd all had with the thunderstorm and it didn't help that my husband had left early to catch the train to London and that I was anxious to collect my thoughts about the book that was being discussed at the club I belong to in Oxford.

'I should explain that Richard always seemed to have a calming effect on Lexie and that morning she was at her most irritating. She and Lizzie were quarrelling about who should have Matthew's share of the fruit salad – he said he had a headache and an upset stomach – and they were having a bit of a tug-of-war over it. I leaned across to take the bowl off them and knocked over the milk jug and broke it. It was clearly Lexie's fault – she was, after all, sixteen and far too old for that sort of behaviour – and I sent her off to her room, while Matthew went to ask our housekeeper to clear up the mess. I decided to leave her to it and, in any case, she had already agreed to take Lizzie up to my mother, who has a small flat on the first floor and who kindly always looks after her when I am out.

'I have to admit that the whole incident put me in a foul temper and I went into my study to have a last look at the notes on what I might say at the book club I was going to that morning. I wasn't due to lead the discussion or anything, but I like to have some idea of what aspects of the book I might bring up myself. To be honest I was also already getting more than a bit worked up about the meeting next week, when I am due to give a formal, video illustrated talk about dressage, to do with both performance and training. It is to be held at the new centre, a few miles this side of Oxford, which has all the facilities and also a restaurant. The other members have kindly offered to give a lunch for me after my talk, which I really appreciate. To be honest, I have been regretting having agreed to do it for some time and even thought of cancelling in view of what has happened here. I've never been one to shirk a challenge, though, and in the long run, I'm sure I'll be glad that I did it, once it's over. I know perfectly well, from my previous experience of competitions, that it's a waste of time worrying in advance, but even so I have to admit that the very thought of it had got to me and I was even in a bit of a state on the day that that awful thing happened to Lexie. There was no particular reason for it and I think it was just due to being reminded of the ordeal ahead.'

'You have had quite a bit of experience of eventing, have you?'

'Yes, dressage. You see, I represented England at the European Championships some years ago and I thought the group would be interested in the training that one had to do with the horse, the different steps that had to be carried out and the stress of important competitions. You asked about the time I left here last Tuesday. Now I come to think about it, although I don't know exactly, it must have been fairly soon after nine, because, even though I stopped for petrol at Blake's garage just up the road on the way, I got there in good time.'

'So, after the incident at breakfast, you didn't see anyone before you left.'

'No, I didn't.'

'Did the book club go well?'

'It could have been worse, but I wasn't concentrating very well, perhaps because I couldn't get the thought of the ordeal ahead out of my mind.'

'Did you get very nervous before the dressage competitions?'

'Yes, I did, but once I was on the horse and we got going, I was all right. What happened to Lexie is quite different, though, and I'm not sure that I'll ever get over that.'

'Thank you for being so frank. Perhaps we might have a word with your mother, now.'

'Is that really necessary? She is getting on a bit, is rather frail and is already very upset at the moment.'

'Yes, we fully realize that she must be,' Sinclair said, 'but we can't afford to miss any possible line of inquiry and Alex may just possibly have confided in her in some way or other, particularly after she came back from Corfu. Perhaps it would be best if my colleague saw her on her own and I'll go into the grounds and have a look round as well as talking to the gardener and the boy who helps him. Is he back at work yet after the terrible shock he must have had?'

'Yes, he is. Phil doesn't get on with his father, who, to be honest, is not a nice man. He's a bully and has a ferocious temper and there are rumours that he hits his wife, and Phil for that matter, when he's had too much to drink. He works on one of the neighbouring farms. Fred, our gardener, who's not married, is very good to Phil, acting as a sort of surrogate grandfather – he must be well into his sixties – and he thought it best for him to get back to work straight away rather than dwell too much on what had happened.'

'Right, thank you again. As I mentioned earlier, we will be coming back after lunch with the people from Oxford to look at Alex's room.'

As the two detectives had already decided that Sarah should see Mrs Carlyle on her own, Mark Sinclair decided to take the opportunity to have a walk around the grounds and Sarah was sitting alone when Mrs Carlyle came into the drawing room. Sarah's first impression of Lexie's grandmother was that she most certainly was neither frail, nor upset. As she came into the drawing room with her daughter, Sarah rose from the armchair and the woman advanced briskly towards her, gave her a firm handshake and introduced herself.

'Maddy,' she said to her daughter, 'would you kindly ask Mrs Weston to bring us coffee? I'm sure that the inspector would welcome a cup and so, for that matter, would I. There's no need to come back, I know just how busy you are and we can manage perfectly well on our own.'

When her daughter had gone, the woman gave Sarah a broad smile. 'You may be surprised by my somewhat acerbic way of dealing with my daughter, but to tell you the truth, I'm fed up to the back teeth with her considering me to be like some senile old granny, when, particularly as even though I say it myself, I more than pull my weight here. Enough said, in fact it was very good of both her and my son-in-law to take me in after my husband died and I had nowhere else to go – he had squandered all our money in some daft scheme he fell for. I like to think that I've paid them back in spades by doing more than my share of coping with Lexie. I'll explain when the coffee arrives.'

While they were waiting, Mrs Carlyle asked Sarah about her work as a detective and gave it her full attention, listening carefully and asking questions until the housekeeper came in with a cafetière of coffee, a jug of cream and a plate of biscuits.

'I believe that you were in this room with Lizzie when young Phil raised the alarm,' Sarah said when the woman had gone.

'Yes, I was helping her with her knitting when the poor young fellow hammered on the terrace door. He was in a terrible state, soaking wet and almost incoherent. I got the housekeeper to look after Lizzie and went down to the pool with him. As soon as I had seen that there was nothing to be done for poor Lexie, I brought him back to the house and after I had rung for the police and the ambulance people, I got Mrs Weston to run a bath for him and find him some dry clothes.'

'I gathered from your daughter that Alex was something of a handful,' Sarah said after she had taken some sips of her coffee.

'She certainly was. She was always highly emotional, either high as a kite, or in the depths of misery and it got worse with adolescence, which came early for her. To be thoroughly indiscreet, Maddy's rigid religious views didn't help in that regard, particularly over matters of sex, which she seems only too ready to equate with sin, something which I gather is not all that rare in Anglo-Catholics, one of which she likes to call herself, and that is something that I personally abhor.

'Maddy is not the most patient of women and I'm sorry to

have to say that until fairly recently she was also in the habit of spanking Alex when she was being particularly tiresome, something which I considered quite unacceptable in the present social climate.

'The last occasion she did that was when she discovered Lexie pleasuring herself, as she coyly put it, when she went to say goodnight to her one evening a few months ago. She gave her a lengthy harangue about how sinful it was, and that she must pray for forgiveness and that the filthy practice must be resisted with prayer. After that, she really laid into her with the back of a clothes brush. It was the housekeeper, Mrs Weston, who had heard what was going on. She told me about it and I was really shocked when I saw the evidence of it myself. Madeleine and I had a major row about it and I told that what she had done was unacceptable, even against the law and that I had a good mind to tell Richard about it. That really shook her and she retaliated by saying if I knew so much about dealing with a difficult adolescent girl like Lexie, then she was only too happy to let me do so.'

'And that's what happened, was it?'

'Yes, but it didn't make that much difference to me as I was already doing most of it already.'

'But you didn't tell your son-in-law about what your daughter had done to Alex?'

'No, I felt I had gone as far as I could. I do worry about Maddy. You will have gathered already that I don't hold with either my daughter's ideas about child rearing or some of her religious views. I have been concerned that she might even wish to formalize her religious views particularly after she had been so taken up with the Pope's visit last year. Were she to do so, I'm quite sure that it would cause all sorts of problems with both Richard and his father.'

'Does her husband know about that possibility?'

'I very much doubt it. As you may imagine, I am in a difficult position over this as I have no religious beliefs at all myself and in my position here I feel it would be quite wrong to stick my oar into such a delicate matter such as that. Richard has always been most friendly towards me and appreciative of what I do here and I would certainly not do anything to prejudice my excellent relationship with him.'

'How did the housekeeper find out about Alex's beating?'

'Mrs Weston's bedroom is quite close to that of Alex and she heard Madeleine shouting at her and then the sound of it. After Maddy had gone, she went in to see if Lexie was all right and found her looking at her backside in the mirror. She wasn't crying and put a brave face on it, saying that she was fine, but Mrs Weston was so shocked by what she had seen that she felt she had to do something about it. The reason she came to me was that she was frightened of losing her job if she went straight to either Maddy or Richard.'

'When did all that take place?'

'Earlier this year.'

'Was Alex very upset by it?'

The woman smiled. 'Not a bit. She even boasted that it hadn't hurt all that much, but after having seen the result I certainly didn't believe her.'

'How have your relations been with your daughter since all that happened?'

'Frosty would be the best description. I got the impression that she would have liked to get rid of both me and Alex, for that matter, but I'm quite sure she was too frightened of Richard's reaction if she pursued that line.'

'How do you get on with Sir Michael?'

'Very well. He is such a nice and charming man. I have to say, something of a contrast to his late wife, who died not all that long ago. To my way of thinking, she was both humourless and more than a bit of a prude. Sir Michael is very good with Lexie, too. He lives not far from her school, of which he is Chairman of the Board of Governors, and takes her out for Sunday lunch with her friend from time to time.'

'What was your son-in-law's attitude to Lexie after the Corfu episode?'

'He told you about that affair, did he?'

'Yes, he did.'

'I was most impressed by the way he handled her when he brought her back here. In my presence, without making a great drama of it, he explained to her that what she had been doing out there was, at her age, against the law, which had been made for good reasons. He also went on to explain that there were obvious dangers of infection and an unwanted pregnancy following behaviour of that sort at her age and that there was ample evidence that it didn't lead to happiness in the future, let alone the increased risk of cancer of the cervix in those who started having intercourse when very young. He said he realized that some people had very strong sexual impulses, which made it more difficult than for those not so troubled in that way and he said that a chat to the GP, a young married woman, would be easier for her than talking to either of us in detail about the subject and that he was going to arrange an appointment with her.'

'How did Alex react to that?'

'Very well, I thought. She listened to what he had to say without the floods of tears that I was expecting, agreed to the visit to the GP and apologized. Richard, very sensibly, in my opinion, left it at that and kept her busy while the others were still in Corfu, helping her with her tennis, which she enjoyed and for which she showed some talent. He also took her to the local aquatics centre as the pool here is unheated and at that time of year still hadn't been filled. Richard was also careful not to leave me out, either. The three of us went to Whipsnade Zoo and altogether it was a happy time.'

'Did you tackle the sex bit with her yourself?'

'No, I thought that Richard's suggestion that the GP should handle that was the best way forward. The little

minx, though, did ask me if I had done it myself at her age.'
The woman smiled. 'I wasn't going to fall for that one and
merely told her that another thing she must learn, and
quickly, was that some matters were private and, provided
that they didn't affect others, that was where they should
remain. I went on to say that it would be best if, as her
father had suggested, she kept her questions for Dr Mead,
the family GP, who would be able to give her accurate information.'

'Do you know if she did that?'

'I know that she went, but you'd have to ask Dr Mead
about the details.'

'Was Lexie attractive physically?'

'I'm sure you know the expression, "beauty is in the eye of
the beholder", but the beholder would have had to be either
very unobservant or else half blind not to have recognized
it in her. The best way of showing you what I mean is to
show you a photo, but that will mean going up to my
bedroom to fetch my album, which perhaps we might do
when we have finished in here. I took the picture when we
got back from Corfu as Alex wanted to show me the bikini
she had bought there without her parents' knowledge. Were
I to get it now, I might have to face an inquisition from my
daughter. Anyway, in my opinion Lexie was an absolute
stunner and she was certainly well aware of it. Poor Phil,
the gardener's boy, whom I know quite well, was smitten by
her; there is no other word for it.'

'Just how smitten, do you think?'

'You mean were they having full intercourse?' Sarah smiled at her and nodded. 'Well, I have no means of knowing, but I very much doubt it. Phil is very shy, has a downtrodden mother and a bully of a father, who used to beat him when he was younger. The man's also a notorious drunkard and, by the look of him, that has already begun to take its toll. I could be wrong, of course, but that isn't to say that Lexie didn't tease Phil in that way. She had told me that she would only wear the bikini for sunbathing by the pool, which is probably where Phil might well have seen her in it, because I saw him coming out of the wood a few days ago when I was picking up some windfall apples, and, how shall I put it?' The woman glanced in Sarah's direction and raised her eyebrows slightly. 'Let me just say that he didn't look exactly comfortable.'

'Do you think he did more than just look at her?'

'I have no doubt that he would have liked to, but as I said, I think it unlikely.'

'What about the gardener?'

'On the outside, Palmer might seem a bit gruff and surly, but I really like him and he certainly really knows his stuff. He's also a brilliant photographer; he takes the most beautiful pictures of flowers; I've got one of his in my room. It's a study of bluebells in the wood and the effect of the sunlight on them through the trees is quite magical. He had also taken numerous pictures of the house, inside and out, as well as the grounds and repeated the exercise after all the alterations had been made. Richard was terribly pleased and had them put in a special album. Very thoughtfully, I thought, too, he gave Palmer matching ones.

'Fred is also very good at fixing all sorts of things, even fiddly ones and you'd never guess that by looking at his hands – they're both big and usually covered with scratches and you should see his nails! To give you an example, I'm always having problems with my electric sewing machine – it's quite tricky to thread the cotton and I'm forever getting it into a tangle. I usually manage to unravel it in the end, but recently it defeated me completely and he dealt with it in no time.'

'I wonder if you'd mind getting that photo of Alex now?' Sarah said. 'I'd like my colleague, Mark Sinclair, to see it, too, and also to introduce him to you at the same time. He's out in the grounds somewhere and it may take me a few minutes to find him. Perhaps we could meet here say in about ten minutes' time.'

'Very well. It's not as if the picture's stuck in to the album, it's behind one of those plastic sheets that one can peel back. I'll get it right away, but in view of what I've already told you, I'd rather you didn't mention to Maddy my showing it to you. I hope you understand.'

Sarah gave her a smile. 'Of course I do. I'll just nip out and fetch Mark; he's out in the grounds somewhere.'

As soon as she was out on the terrace, Sarah saw her

partner walking in the direction of the kitchen garden and managed to intercept him, quickly outlining what Mrs Carlyle had told her about Alex and the photograph.

'That's all very helpful,' he said, 'and after I've met this Mrs Carlyle, I think it would be a good idea if we saw the gardener and his assistant together. But before we do so I'd like to fill you in on my interview with young Matthew Travers.'

Mrs Carlyle was waiting for them in the drawing room and gave Sinclair a warm smile as they shook hands.

'I managed to sneak upstairs without alerting "she who must be obeyed",' she said, holding out the photograph.

'You must, like me, be a devotee of Rider Haggard?' Sinclair said with a smile.

The woman nodded. 'I have "She" in my bookcase in my bedroom and had been reading it to Lexie. I'd forgotten how good it was and she was enthralled by it. My hope was that books like that might fire in her an enthusiasm for reading in general, something which had been sadly lacking in her life. I was explaining to your colleague about Maddy having flirted with the idea of Catholicism and even Opus Dei and needless to say she doesn't approve of that type of book and she almost has an apoplectic fit whenever *The Da Vinci Code* is mentioned, although she has neither read the book nor seen the film, both of which are completely off limits as far as she is concerned. She is also prudish in the extreme and I've often wondered how Richard, who is a very attractive man, puts up with her, now that she's become so pious. She wasn't always like that and I blame her study of the Opus Dei business for it. Now, you won't want me banging on about her, your colleague has heard quite enough about that already and it's the photo you'll be wanting to see.'

In the picture, the girl was wearing a straw hat and was smiling at the camera. Stunning was the only word to describe her, Sinclair thought. The smile she had for her grandmother was obviously genuine and her skimpy bikini set off her slim, but well developed figure, to perfection.

'No wonder the young fellow in Corfu got carried away,' he said. 'Do you know whether the two of them went the whole way, or not?'

'My son-in-law was rather coy about that when telling me about it, but I can well understand if the young Greek boy wasn't able to restrain himself. It is equally obvious that Phil, the gardener's boy, feels exactly the same about her, but, as I told your colleague, I believe he's far too shy and inhibited to have done anything about it.'

After thanking the woman, the two detectives strolled across the lawn towards the trees with the kitchen garden to their right.

'Why don't we sit down over there in the shade?' Sinclair said. 'I'd like to tell you about young Matthew Travers and you can give me an impression of Mrs Carlyle. Why don't you go first?'

Sarah described how the woman had come to live with

the family and about her reaction to Alex's beating. 'She seems to like her son-in-law and even more his father, but she obviously believes that her daughter was, to some extent, responsible for Lexie's difficulties and you heard her say how prudish she had become. It also appears that she lacks a sense of humour and had no idea how to handle the girl, particularly with regard to sex.'

Sarah explained that Mrs Carlyle was obviously quite clear in her mind that her daughter's previous spanking of Alex and the one occasion when it amounted to quite a severe beating with the back of a wooden clothes brush was unacceptable, not least for the reason she did it.

'Would you go as far as to suspect that Madeleine Travers might have been responsible for Alex's death?'

'I think that's very unlikely, but we clearly need another account of what happened at the breakfast table that morning. I also thought it would be worth checking at the garage, where she told me that she had filled her car up the morning it all happened. If she paid by credit or debit card, the exact time would be on the receipt and if we are able to discover if Alex went down to the pool after that, the woman would be in the clear.

'I got no hint about her relationship with her husband, but if Madeleine is as uptight about sex as her mother implied, then that would reinforce our suspicions about Richard Travers's relationship with his secretary. There is no doubt that Mrs Carlyle gets on well with her son-in-law and the two of them obviously handled Lexie both sympathetically and effectively when he brought her back from Corfu.

'It's not difficult to imagine what a shock to her system the adoption of Alex must have been to Madeleine Travers, considering the way the girl turned out as she got older, and I have little doubt that latterly she must have regretted the decision to have done it, particularly after she had unexpectedly produced the pretty, biddable daughter that Lizzie has proved to be. Alex must have been a nightmare for her: highly emotional, in her mother's eyes unstable and latterly obsessed with sex, the last straw must have been the incident in Corfu and, harsh though it is to say, I can't help feeling that in the long run the girl's death may well prove to be a relief to her. Perhaps, not even in the long run, because she did not give me the impression of being someone overwhelmed by grief. There is no doubt, too, that Alex must have been a handful and a half and we should certainly get the GP's view and that of her school. There seems to have been trouble there, too.'

Sinclair nodded. 'I was rather impressed by Travers and he seems to have handled the Corfu incident pretty well.'

'I agree, but I wonder if the thought of a pliant younger woman awaiting him in his office made the idea of bringing Lexie back to the UK such an attractive one?'

Sinclair raised his eyebrows. 'I wouldn't be surprised.'

'How did you get on with young Matthew?'

'He's a rather odd boy in many ways, old before his time is as good a way of describing him as any other. He speaks in a curiously stilted and outdated way, rather like the heroes of some of the pre-war authors of adventure stories such as those written by Dornford Yates and Sapper, of which my father had a store and which I liked to read when I was Matthew's age. Let me explain.'

THREE

THE TENNIS COURT was in a corner of the garden hidden by a screen of trees and as it came into view, Sinclair heard the familiar sound of the click of a golf ball as it was hit, followed by a muffled curse. The tall, slim figure put another ball on the tee and another wild swipe sent the ball straight into the side netting, which had been set up next to the court.

'I hope you won't mind if I give you a hint,' Sinclair said.

He young man whirled round. 'Who the hell are you?' he said, flushing angrily.

'My name is Sinclair, Inspector Sinclair. I'm one of the detectives looking into the sad death of your sister and you must be Matthew. No doubt your father warned you that we would be coming.'

Before he had time to reply, Sinclair walked towards him, took a three wood out of the golf bag, picked a ball out of the bucket and put it on the tee peg. Pausing only for a moment, he settled into his stance and took an easy swing; there was a sharp click and the ball slammed into the back netting some ten paces straight ahead of him.

'There's nothing wrong with your grip and stance, but you're not swinging the club through the ball, you're hitting from the top and lifting your head as well. It is essential to keep that as still as possible until after impact.'

He demonstrated another couple of shots, first mimicking the young man's efforts and then executing a further perfect drive.

'Why don't you have another try, this time with this three wood. It's easier to use than the driver.'

Two or three shots later, there was the sound of the face of the club connecting perfectly with the ball, which went off like a tracer bullet.

'Excellent, well done. With a bit more practice and with your height, you'll soon be hitting your drives well over two hundred yards. Why not have a few lessons first with your local professional? He will be much better at putting you on the right track and detecting faults than I am and it's much easier to start that way, rather than trying to correct existing errors. Anyway, let's sit down over there.'

Still looking distinctly shell-shocked, the young man allowed himself to be directed to the bench just inside the hut where the tennis and golf equipment was housed.

'I'm sure that the last thing you want to talk about is your sister, Alex, but equally you must realize that we have to find out who did that terrible thing to her. I already understand from my conversation with your father that she was something of a problem.'

The young man flushed. 'A problem! I am a committed Christian, Inspector, as are my parents, and I believe in both good and evil and Alexandra was evil, truly evil.'

'In what way?'

'She was a wicked temptress. She flaunted her body in front of everyone, women as well as men, and committed the sin of fornication with that boy in Corfu. There was also an incident with a girl at her school – I couldn't help over-hearing my parents discussing it.'

'And did she embarrass you in that way, herself?'

The young man flushed. 'She took a delight in teasing me by walking around half naked in my presence, and asking me, on one occasion, to undo the knot at the back of her bikini top, which she said that she had tied too tight. The strip of material also just happened to fall off when I had loosened it. I knew exactly what she wanted me to do to her and it was a sore trial to me. I'm not made of wood and had it not been for my faith, I might well have succumbed.'

'Did you mention any of this to your parents?'

'I did have a talk to my father, but to be honest he wasn't able to help all that much. He just said that girls as well as boys often had difficulties when they were growing up and the best thing to do if she did carry out silly tricks like the one I described, was to walk away and ignore them.' The young man shook his head. 'What she did was not a silly trick, at least not to me – I found it very upsetting. Last term, I mentioned it the assistant chaplain at my school and that helped me quite a lot.'

'What did he say?'

'Just that I must be strong and that temptations were made to be overcome and that I must pray for her to see the error of her ways and change them.' He took out his handkerchief and pretended to blow his nose. 'I did pray for her and then that awful thing had to happen.'

'Where were you before and when she was found by the gardener's boy?'

'You don't think....'

'That is a question we have to ask everyone who was here at the time. Someone might have noticed something out of the ordinary and any clue could be helpful.'

'I'm sorry, I do understand. I wasn't feeling at all well at breakfast that morning and went into the downstairs cloakroom as I was feeling sick. After a bit, I went upstairs to lie down in my bedroom and had a short sleep. When I woke I was feeling quite a lot better and went for a stroll in the grounds. Lizzie showed me the plant she was growing for our grandmother's birthday. It was not long after that that Phil found Lexie in the pool.'

'Tell me about your younger sister, Lizzie.'

'She can be a bit of a nuisance with her constant questions, but she's a really nice little girl, always cheerful, happy and enthusiastic. I read to her quite a lot – she's only seven, but is already heavily into *Harry Potter* – and I'm helping her with tennis, which she has just started. She has lots of friends at her primary school and she often goes round to their houses to play with them. My grandmother is wonderful with her. She also helps with her reading and is teaching her to knit and do needlework. She was also the only person here who knew how to handle Alex without provoking dramatic scenes. She has always been there for us, me included, ever since she came to live with us after my grandfather died, it must have been about ten years ago.

The one thing that worries me about her is that she doesn't believe in religion. I asked her once why that was and she just smiled and said: "As I'm sure you know, your mother became very taken up with it after she met your father and they became engaged to be married. It was obviously the right decision for her and she has never had any doubts about it since, nor have I had any problems with accepting her new beliefs. As for me, I'm sure you know the expression 'being happy in one's own skin'. Well, I am quite happy in not believing in God and by the same token I never challenge or fail to respect other people's way of thinking. I sometimes wish that people were more tolerant and that applies as much to atheists as to the religious and I do understand that strong beliefs are important to many people. My views are not exactly popular around here, particularly with your mother and some members of your father's family, who are very certain about their faith. As for your father and grandfather, they have had much more experience of life than the others and are more tolerant. I'm well aware that you have strong views about it yourself and there is nothing wrong with that".'

'Your grandmother sounds to be a lovely person,' Sinclair said.

'Yes, she is, but, as I said, I do worry about her and her lack of religious belief and I often pray for her.'

'Do you get on well with your grandfather?'

'I don't see him all that often, but he is always very friendly when I do and interested to hear how I am getting on. He was very good with Alex. I don't know how he did it, but she seemed quite different with him, never being rude or grumpy in his presence.'

'Tell me about the gardener and his assistant.'

'Phil's all right, but I can't stand Palmer.'

'Why not? What's wrong with him?'

'He's an old grouch and thinks he owns the garden and is always complaining about something.'

'What sort of thing?'

'I had been doing some putting on the back lawn and failed to notice that I had left a ball there. You've never heard such a carry on. It might have damaged the mower, there was a perfectly good golf range with a putting green within easy cycling distance of the house and so on. On another occasion, he had a go at me for failing to slacken the net on the tennis court after I had been practising my serve. I didn't like the way he used to look at Lexie, either.'

'In what way was that exactly?'

'It was partly her fault. She would walk around the garden wearing that ridiculous bikini of hers and whenever she did, he couldn't keep his eyes off her. There was another occasion, too, when that silly friend of hers from school came to stay here. They liked to sunbathe by the pool and, you've guessed it, he just had to check the state of the trees down there and was carrying his camera at the time. He takes a lot of photographs of the flowers and I must say they are brilliant; he does his own developing and printing in his house and I couldn't help wondering if he was taking pictures of them, too.'

'Did he know that you had seen him on that occasion?'

'No, I'm sure he didn't as he was walking away from me with his camera strap over his shoulder.'

'How's school for you?'

'I can't wait to leave.'

'Why's that?'

'I've grown out of it, I suppose.'

'How much longer have you got there?'

'One more year.'

'"A" levels coming up?'

'Yes.'

'What subjects are you taking?'

'English, history and religious studies.'

Sinclair smiled at the boy and got to his feet. 'Nice to have met you. I have to go now. Good luck with the golf.'

Matthew Travers gave the detective a shy smile. 'What you told me about that, sir, was very helpful and I see that I'll have to persuade my father to let me have some lessons.'

'Good idea. It's a great game and one which people, women as well as men, can play with great enjoyment until old age. I wouldn't say this to everyone, because I don't think it would go down well with a lot of people I know, who would think it unutterably pompous, but I believe that golf teaches one a lot about life, too. How to take the rough with the smooth, how to win graciously and accept defeat in the same spirit.'

Sinclair left Matthew Travers feeling slightly shell-shocked. He had found the boy's manner and a lot of what he had said stilted and even middle-aged – he had even found himself speaking in the same way himself, for God's sake! Did the boy really believe it all himself, or was it an echo of someone at his school? He couldn't believe that it came from his father, who had given the impression of being worldly in the extreme, or his mother for that matter. What he had said about the gardener was interesting, though, but was it true? It was only too clear, though, how much young Travers disliked him.

'Why don't you wait here a moment, Sarah?' Sinclair said when he had finished telling her about Matthew Travers, 'and I'll find the gardener's boy and bring him over so that we can have a chat to him before the scene-of-crime fellow shows us where Lexie was found.'

'Good idea.'

As he went into the kitchen garden Sinclair immediately spotted a young fellow, who was weeding a vegetable patch.

'Hello,' he said, 'you must be Phil. My name is Sinclair and I'm one of the detectives looking into the sad death of Alex Travers. My colleague and I would like to have a word with you about how you found her.'

The young man, who appeared to the detective to be in his middle to late teens, looked anxiously over his shoulder. 'I'd better tell Mr Palmer first, sir.'

'Hard taskmaster, is he?'

'He's all right, sir, just a bit strict.'

'Is that him over there?'

'Yes, sir.'

'Don't worry, I'll have a quick word with him myself.'

Sinclair came back almost straight away and gave the boy a smile. 'That's all fixed. My colleague is sitting on the seat at the bottom of the lawn over there.'

The wide wooden seat had plenty of room for three people and was out of sight of both the gardener and the house. After Sinclair had introduced him to Sarah, the young man gradually gained confidence once the interview had begun.

'First of all,' Sinclair said with a smile, 'would you tell me what time you came in to work the morning it all happened.'

'Normal like, we always start work at eight o'clock, but that morning I had to go to the dentist. My appointment was at nine o'clock, but there were a bit of a delay and I didn't get here until nearly ten. Mr Palmer had been having a cup of tea with Mrs Parsmore while waiting for me and he must have seen me arrive on me bike, because he came out to meet me. He were a bit grumpy 'cos I were so late and he told me to go straight down to the wood to see if any branches had come down near the pool during the thunderstorm the night before, when there were a high wind an' all.'

'Did you go down there straight away?'

'I had to get the saw, the chopper and the wheelbarrow, so it took me a bit of time to get going, like.'

'Roughly when was that?'

'Must have been about twenty past ten.'

'And there was a lot of damage down in the wood, was there?'

'Yeah. Quite a bit.'

The boy described how, after he had been working for about half an hour, he was feeling hot and sweaty and went along the path to the pond through the wood to dip his hands and head into the water.

'She were lying face down under the water,' he said, obviously trying hard not to cry.

'She had no clothes on, I understand,' Sinclair said.

The boy nodded and a flush spread all over his face and he was hardly able to get his next words out.

'Yes. I jumped in and when I lifted her head up, I could

see her face were all smashed in. I got her out an' she weren't breathing, so I tried to get it going.'

'What exactly did you do?'

'We'd been shown it at school.'

'You mean artificial respiration?'

'Yes. I tried, I really did, but it were no good, what with her nose being broke and some of her teeth loose. After I'd been doing it for a few minutes and she still wasn't breathing, I just knew she were dead, so I ran up to the house. Mrs Carlyle were there and she were ever so good. She went down to the pool with me, told me that I'd done everything possible and then she took me back to the house, rang for an ambulance, and asked Mrs Weston to fill a bath for me and give me dry clothes to put on.

'One of the coppers, who had also come, told Mrs Carlyle she shouldn't have let me change me clothes and she gave him a right telling off.'

'What exactly did she say?'

'That I'd done me best for the girl and did they want me to be rewarded by catching me death of cold? She were really angry.'

Tears were running down his cheeks and Sinclair took his handkerchief out of the breast pocket of his jacket, handed it to the boy and watched as he dabbed his eyes and then shook his head, before handing it back.

'You did everything possible, Phil,' Sinclair said, putting his arm round the boy's shoulders. 'We are quite sure that

Alex was already dead when you found her in the water. Has anyone spoken to you about it apart from Mrs Carlyle?'

'Mr Travers did. He was very nice to me an' all, thanking me and saying that I'd done me best for Lexie and no one else could have done more.'

'How about Fred Palmer?'

'He didn't say much, but after I'd had me bath and Mrs Carlyle told the cook to give me some lunch, he said I could go home if I liked. My clothes were dry by then and I told him I'd rather do some work and he just nodded and got me to cut up some of the wood to put on the bonfire and while I was doing that, he got the fire going with some twigs. He were real nice to me.'

'How do you get on with Lizzie?'

'She's a really nice little girl. She always thanks me for pushing her on the swing and helping her to grow things in her small plot.'

Sinclair looked at the young man very directly, who met his eyes for a few moments and then his gaze dropped.

'Alex was more than just a pretty girl to you, wasn't she, Phil?'

There was a long silence and then tears filled the boy's eyes and began to run slowly down his cheeks.

'Why not tell us about it, all of it?' Sinclair handed him his handkerchief again and watched as the boy dried his eyes. 'Take your time and if you tell us the absolute truth, there'll be no need for you to worry about getting into trouble or us passing it on to her parents. You do want us to find out who did that terrible thing to Alex, don't you?'

Phil Carter looked at the detective for a moment or two and then nodded. 'You won't say anything to Mr Travers or my dad, either, will you? He'll kill me if he finds out.'

'That you had had sex with Alex? No, we won't tell him that.'

From the moment that he had started working for the Travers family the previous year, Phil Carter had hardly been able to take his eyes off the girl. She was so pretty, such fun, always with a smile and always stopping to have a word with him when she saw him in the garden. It wasn't only that; he had never even seen a girl of her age wearing nothing more than a couple of thin strips of material, let alone within touching distance. She would appear when he was working on his own, with Fred Palmer well out of sight. He remembered the occasions when he was trimming the edges of the lawn or weeding in the rose garden, that he'd heard something and looked round to see her smiling at him, usually wearing very short shorts and a thin shirt, through which he was able to make out the fascinating shapes underneath.

It happened one day only a few weeks before the terrible events surrounding her death. There was no one else in the grounds, Fred having gone off to the big gardening centre near Oxford to look at lawn mowers, saying that the old one was well past its best and constantly breaking down. Mr Travers was in his office in the village; Mrs Travers and her mother were also out, attending a coffee morning to raise funds for equipment for the local primary school; Matthew was, as usual, shut up in his room, working for his 'A' levels and Lizzie was at a friend's house. Phil was on his knees doing some digging, when he heard a sound behind him and looked round to see Alex, who was standing only a couple of feet away, carrying a large bathing towel.

'Would you be an angel, Phil, and help me with the door to the summerhouse? It's got stuck and I want to take the rug and the sunshade down to the pool in case it gets too hot.'

'Of course, Miss Alex.'

'Come on, Phil, we're friends aren't we? My friends always call me Lexie.'

He hardly knew where to look. The tie of her robe had come loose and in the gap at the front he saw that she was wearing only the briefest of brief bikinis, to go with her straw hat and sandals. He was quite unable to take his eyes off her, she was just so pretty.

One sharp pull was enough to free the door and although she could easily have carried the equipment herself, there was no question of his letting her do so.

'I'll give you a hand, if you like.'

'Would you, Phil? You're a star.'

She laid the rug down on the patch of grass in front of the pool, while he raised the sunshade for her and when he turned towards her, he saw her standing on it with bare feet smiling at him.

'Would you like to look at me, Phil? All of me? Don't worry, there's no one else in the garden. I've checked.'

He felt himself flushing and unable to speak, nodded. She undid the tie on her robe, took it off, then her hands went up behind her and the bikini top came away too. There were pictures of topless girls in the magazines in the chest of drawers in his father's bedroom and Phil had often sneaked in when the man was down at the pub and had a long look at them, but they were nothing compared with what he was seeing now.

He was to relive what happened next, time and time again and would never forget it. She was so gentle with him, so patient and he was left in no doubt that she had enjoyed it, all of it, as much as he had, if not more.

When it was all over, they both slowly relaxed and lay side by side, holding each other gently, and he drifted off to sleep.

He woke to see her standing up beside him and smiling down at him. 'Come on, Phil, wakey, wakey. Just time for a quick dip.'

They splashed about in the pool for a few minutes and then she took hold of his hand and pulled him out.

'Back to the weeds with you, Phil. Mr Palmer may come

looking for you when he comes back and I'm expecting the others soon as well.'

'When can I see you again?'

'We'll have to wait until I get back from school. I've got to go there next week and until then my mother won't leave me alone, fussing about the packing and everything.'

'And was that the only occasion on which you had full sex with her?' Sinclair asked.

Phil Carter nodded, tears in his eyes. 'Who could've done such a terrible thing to her? She was such a lovely girl and really nice with it.'

'That's what we're determined to find out. That thunderstorm happened some time later, the night before you found her drowned in the pond. Is that right?'

'Yes. That morning it was warm and sunny again and, as I told you, after I got in, Mr Palmer sent me down to the wood to see if there were any fallen branches and that's when I saw her under the water.' The boy shook his head. 'It was the first time I'd seen her after what we did together.'

'Right,' Sinclair said. 'Have you said anything to anyone apart from us about having sex with Alex, even boasted to a pal about it?'

The boy shook his head violently. 'I'd never do that.'

'You have to keep it that way. If you've got any worries, or think of anything else that might help us, we're the two people you must come to and on no account tell anyone else what happened, not anyone in the Travers family, nor you mum or dad and certainly not Palmer. Is that quite clear?' The boy nodded. 'Oh, by the way, do you happen to know the name of the centre that deals with your mower? My mother, who lives near here, has trouble with hers and if I have time, I'd like to look one out for her.'

'Yes, it's Jessops. It's on the Abingdon road and you can't miss it.'

'What was that about?' Sarah asked, as they watched the boy as he walked away from them across the lawn without looking back.

'You remember that the day that Phil was making love with Lexie, Palmer was supposed to be looking at mowers for Travers?' Sarah nodded. 'Well, you see, Matthew told me that the man was always wandering around the grounds with his camera, photographing flowers and I wonder if that morning he decided to see if he could get some shots of the two young people at it. He must surely have noticed that young Phil couldn't take his eyes off the girl and might have taken that opportunity to spy on them, knowing that everyone except the cook, who never goes out into the garden, was out. It's a bit of a long shot, but I might as well check the garden centre out. What did you make of young Phil?'

'I was rather impressed by him and I thought he was telling us the truth.'

'I agree. Why not let us have a word with the gardener

fellow and then I think a spot of lunch would be in order? The scene-of-crime bloke's not due until two, which'll give us a good hour and a half.'

'Good idea,' Sarah said. 'Probably makes sense to go to a pub some way away; I reckon if we turn up at the local one, it'll only add to the gossip, which is no doubt in full flow already.'

They found Fred Palmer in the long tool shed at one side of the vegetable garden, sharpening the blade of a scythe.

'This sad business must have caused a lot of upset to the household,' Sinclair said, when he had made the introductions.

'Yes, sir, it did.'

'Been here some time, have you?'

'Best part of forty year. Mind, it were a lot quieter when old Mrs Forrest were here on her own with her companion.'

'When did the Traverses arrive?'

'Gone ten year, I reckon.'

'Made a lot of changes, did they?'

'Yes. I know about the house 'cos I have done quite a few odd jobs in there over the years, and old Mrs Forest wouldn't have recognized it, so different did it become. As for the grounds, the old croquet lawn were removed and a hard tennis court put there instead, with a swimming pool just beyond it. The old stables were turned into garages.'

'What about the small pool at the bottom of the garden where Phil found the girl?'

'There always was a patch of grass down there in front of it and the previous owner, Mrs Forrest, used to get me to push her down there in her wheelchair with her house-keeper, who helped her to settle and then left her there sitting in a low chair, usually for about an hour – the wood hadn't grown up so much then and the path was wider. She liked to sit there with a book and if it were very hot, she'd put her swollen feet in the water. It were private, like, down there in them days and no one could see her.'

'You may have been told that Alex Travers's clothes and towel were found on that large flat stone on the other side of the pond. Do you know when that rock was first put there?'

The man shrugged his shoulders. 'It were there when I first came here, but the pool were shallower in them days. Mr Travers got some blokes to come here with a digger to make it both deeper and bigger.'

'When we first came into the grounds, we were struck by the stone wall leading away from both sides of the main gates; does it go right round the property?'

'Yes, an' Phil or I check it every week, in case the vandals had got at it. Very particular Mr Travers is about it. Bits of it had fallen down when they first came here and he had it fixed up proper when they moved in. Two new sets of new gates were set into it.'

'Do you get on well with the Travers family?'

'I don't see all that much of Mr Travers, as he's often

away in London, but he always has a word with me when he comes into the garden. His missus isn't in the garden much, either, but her mother, Mrs Carlyle, takes a real interest, like, and she knows her flowers and plants right enough. She's a real good sort.'

'And the children?'

'Matthew thinks he's already lord of the manor, right snooty bugger he is an' all, and that Alex! My old gran always used to say that you mustn't speak ill of the dead, but a right slag, she was. Even though she were younger than Phil, she were always showing off her whatsits, like a page three girl and upsetting him.'

'Did Phil complain about her to you?'

The man shook his head. 'Nah, but I could see he was bothered by her. He's too young for that sort of thing and it weren't fair.'

'Did you say anything to Mrs Carlyle about her?'

'It isn't my place to talk to anyone in the family about things like that.'

'What about the younger girl, Lizzie?'

'She's a bit of a nuisance, always asking questions, but she's a nice little thing and Phil likes her, too. He's always happy to give her a push on the swing and help her with her plot.'

'Have you any idea who might have wanted to harm Alex?'

'The wall isn't that high and perhaps a tramp had been

sleeping in the wood, saw her with nothing on and tried to have a go with her.'

'We need to know where everyone was that morning, as I'm sure you understand. What time did you get in yourself?'

'Normal like, I'm here soon after eight, but knowing that Phil would be late because of the dentist, I came in that day not far short of 9.15. Mrs Parsmore, the cook, was putting some rubbish out as I came in, saw me arriving on me bike and gave me a mug of tea in the kitchen. She's very good like that and I stayed there talking to her about the thunderstorm and that, until through the window I saw Phil coming in through the back gates – it must have been nearly ten by then. I thought we ought to check if any branches had come down in the storm and I sent him down there. When he came back and told me that there was quite a bit of damage, I sent him back down with the chopper and a saw, while I started the bonfire.'

'What time was that?'

'Must have been not far off eleven.'

'Well, thank you, Mr Palmer. Let us know if you think of anything else. One or both of us will be here for the next few days.'

FOUR

AFTER LUNCH, THE two detectives returned to the house and were sitting on the terrace facing the lawn, when the scene-of-crime man, Reg Waters, drove up in his car.

'Good to see you again, sir,' he said as he shook hands with Sinclair.

'And you, Reg. May I introduce my colleague, Inspector Sarah Prescott? We've been working together since I was transferred to the Met.'

'Pleased to meet you, ma'am.'

'As I expect you already know, Reg, we've been briefed by Dr Rawlings and have already had the opportunity to meet all the Travers family here, with the exception of their younger daughter, Lizzie, as well as the gardener and the boy who helps him, Phil Carter. The latter told us how he came to find the girl under the water in the pool and what he did to try to revive her. I've got the photographs here, but we've not been down there yet and perhaps, as a start, you'd give us a conducted tour.'

'Right, sir. We were called in within an hour or so of the

girl having been found and taped off the whole of the small wood. Perhaps the best thing to do first would be to follow the route the gardener's boy took when he had been told to clear the fallen branches, which had come down during the storm the previous night.'

The man led them across the lawn and along the narrow path into the wood.

'Evidently he'd been working for about forty-five minutes that morning, heaping up some of the fallen wood into that pile over there and using his axe to release the loose bits that hadn't been fractured completely. At about eleven, feeling thirsty, he decided to push his way through to the pond to have a drink and cool down by splashing some water on to his face and that's when he found the girl. Let's go down there, shall we, sir? Ma'am?'

The path had been largely trampled down by the passage of the ambulance men and the police and it took them only a short time to reach the grass area in front of the pool.

'I understand that you've already seen Dr Rawlings, so I won't go over the girl's appearance, or precisely where she was found, but if you'd care to follow me, you'll see that it's quite easy to reach the other side. The stream to our left which feeds the pond has numerous rocks in it, which can be used as stepping stones.'

Reg Waters led the way through the gaps in the trees and across the stream and they climbed onto the large flat boulder that was about two-and-a-half feet above the edge of the pool on that side.

'It seems most likely that the girl was lying face down on a towel, sunbathing and reading a book, which we found beside the stone. We believe that she must have heard something behind her, got up and turned to face her assailant. She was then either hit with some weapon or other, or punched in the face. The blow was violent enough to have fractured her nose, injured her left eye and loosened a couple of teeth. She then appears to have fallen over sideways to her right, hitting the edge of the boulder with her right shoulder, before dropping face down into the water. She was almost certainly unconscious when she landed there.'

'Any evidence of an intruder having got over the wall behind this boulder?'

'No, sir, but it wouldn't have been difficult to climb over it in any number of places as it's not all that high. It's constructed of stone, which is in good condition and goes right round the property with two sets of gates; the main ones, through which you must have driven, are made of metal and there is a second set of wooden ones, used by trade vehicles at the back. Both sets are connected by bells and a speaker to the kitchen and can be opened from there electronically. We've been round the whole of the wall with the gardener and there is no evidence of anyone having climbed over it recently, although it's impossible to be absolutely sure.'

'How much damage was done to the wood in the gale?'

'Nothing major, although quite a few small branches had come down, which the boy was clearing before he found the girl. According to him, the path itself was not completely obstructed and the girl would have had no trouble in getting down to the pool that way even in the sandals she was wearing. Inevitably, though, the ambulance men went charging down it and by the time we got there it was impossible to tell if anyone other than the girl and the gardener's boy had been that way earlier on.'

'Presumably there were no useful footprints on either side of the pond?'

'No, sir, the ambulance men saw to that! The quickest way here from the house is the one we've just taken, but it is also possible to follow the stream that way by stepping from stone to stone until it disappears under the wall surrounding the property through a culvert. When we first inspected the site, following the storm of the previous night, the stream was running a bit higher than it is now, but even so it was quite easy to go that way to the back of the kitchen garden without getting one's feet wet. Would you like me to show you?'

'Yes, please.'

As they followed the course of the stream, they kept catching sight of the wall which encircled the property until they emerged from the wood and saw the water disappearing through the culvert. At that point the wall took a right angle turn to the right and a grassy path separated it from the kitchen garden.

'So with reasonable care,' Sarah said, 'the assailant would have been able to reach the rock, on which the girl was lying, from behind without her being alerted?'

'Yes, ma'am. We got one of the WPCs to lie on the rock in roughly the same position as we assume the girl was in and a man was able to get right up behind her without being heard, any slight noise he might have made being masked by the bubbling sound of the stream. He had, of course, taken every precaution to make his approach as silent as possible and was wearing soft-soled trainers.'

'I don't suppose you found any footmarks on that approach to the boulder.'

The man shook his head. 'Thank you, Reg,' Sinclair said. 'Unless you have any further questions, Sarah, perhaps we should take a look at the girl's room.'

As they walked back towards the house along a path through the kitchen garden, they could hear the sound of wood chopping and then went into the house through the front door.

Waters paused when they were in the hall. 'You might be interested in a brief layout of the house as it now is, quite a few alterations having been made when the Traverses took it on. On the ground floor here, the drawing and dining rooms were redecorated and in addition to them, there is also a small breakfast room, a study which Mrs Travers uses and one other room, which was converted into a play-room for the children and is still used by the youngest one.'

'Does Mr Travers also have a study down here?'

'No, I gather that he uses his office in the town for all his political and personal business. The kitchen block was completely redesigned and now has a cooking and washing up area, a separate room for the heating system and a sitting room for the housekeeper and cook.'

At the head of the staircase, he paused on the landing of the first floor.

'There were four bedrooms on this floor originally; two large ones, one of which had a dressing room attached and two smaller ones. The main one, which has en suite facilities has a view of the lawn and is used by the Traverses; their son, Matthew, has the room over there and the youngest child that one there. They share the second bathroom with Mrs Carlyle, their grandmother. Finally, the second large one and the dressing room have been converted into a small flat for her. She takes her main meals with the family and doesn't have a proper kitchen, but there is a small area in the sitting room in which there is a microwave, a coffee machine and a kettle and that's where she has her breakfast.'

'How many of the other rooms up here are occupied, apart from that of the murdered girl?' Sarah asked, when they had reached the landing on the second floor.

'There are four further bedrooms up here, ma'am; the

dead girl's, those of the housekeeper and the cook and a double spare for guests, with en suite facilities. There is also another bathroom, which contains a shower cubicle as well as the bath and lavatory, and that was shared by the girl and the two domestics.'

'So, altogether, there are six bedrooms, two of which have en suite facilities, plus the granny flat on the two upper floors?' Sarah said.

'Yes, that's right, ma'am.'

The door to the murdered girl's bedroom, immediately to their right on the second floor, had been locked and taped by the scene-of-crime officers and Waters let them in.

'There was no evidence that anyone other than the girl had been in this room on the day of her death,' the man said. 'The housekeeper gives it a thorough clean once a week and had done so three days before the girl's death. Apart from that, the girl was expected to look after it herself.'

Alex Travers's bedroom was in a typical female teenage muddle. There was a duvet and pyjamas in an untidy pile on the bed, which was against the wall on the same side as the door. A variety of clothes were strewn over the floor and a large pin board, attached to the wall to the right of the bed, was covered with posters and cut-outs. Below the pinboard was a desk and chair, on which were a personal computer and a printer and by its side a bookcase. There was a large built-in wardrobe which, together with a chest of drawers, occupied most of the wall opposite the foot of the bed. The windows across the floor from the door looked out onto what had obviously been the stable block, but which had been converted into garages. There was a basin to one side of the windows, with a mirror above it and a cabinet beneath and a dressing table on the other with a three piece mirror and a brush and comb on it. In one of the two small drawers at its base, there were some small items of make-up and in the other a few pieces of costume jewellery, none of which appeared to be of any great value.

'Did you find anything of special interest elsewhere in here, Mr Waters?' Sarah asked.

'She doesn't appear to have kept any correspondence, ma'am, but as you must have seen already there is a collection of postcards and pictures on the pinboard over there. As you have seen, she didn't have a television set. Mrs Travers didn't approve of any of the children sitting for hours in front of one, but for something like sport Matthew used the big set in the drawing room. Mrs Carlyle was not so strict and let the two girls watch hers.

'That wardrobe did contain a number of items, which we decided were best taken away. I have brought them with me, but first I'd like to show you where they were hidden.'

He opened the doors of the wardrobe, one of which had a full length mirror attached to it, revealing a number of drawers to one side, which contained underwear, shirts and pullovers. On a rail to the left were skirts, dresses and coats on hangers and on the floor was a shoe rack.

'The raised floor here is made of plywood and comes out quite easily.'

Waters took out the shoe rack, inserted the blade of his penknife on one side of the wooden base of the wardrobe, lifted up the edge and shone the torch into the cavity underneath, which was empty.

'We thought it best to photograph the contents in situ and then remove them. I have brought them all with me in this suitcase.'

He showed them the picture, then opened his case, lifting out a number of sex aids, a magazine and an illustrated book, all of which he laid out on the top of the girl's desk. 'We also took away her camera and I have some prints taken from it, which we found inside the book and which I also have here. There were several other pictures stored in the camera, which were protected by a password, but our experts were able to access them all.

'I doubt if there is a shop nearer here than Oxford, which is no doubt where she bought the book and the sex aids,' Sarah said. 'Any sign anywhere of drugs, or contraceptives?'

The man shook his head. 'No, ma'am. We looked carefully for any possible hiding places and found nothing like that apart from under the false bottom of the wardrobe.'

'Have you got the photographs here with you?'

'Yes, ma'am, right here.'

Sarah flicked through the prints that Waters had given her and then passed them across to Mark Sinclair. There was one of Alex standing by the pool at the bottom of the garden and a second one of a dark haired girl. Both of them were dressed, if Sinclair thought, one could call it dressed, in miniscule bikinis and were smiling at the camera.

'And here are the images protected by the password.'

The same girls were shown again by the pool, but this time they were posing in ways which left nothing to the imagination, nor did the others, which had been taken on a beach and featured Alex and this time a young man.

'Doubtless he is the son of the proprietor of the hotel in Corfu,' Sinclair said, showing her another view of the same young man, this time from short range, with him rowing a boat.

'Were there any other photos apart from the ones you've shown us?'

'Only the ones in an album in that bookcase over there. They are mainly snaps of the family in the garden and on holiday and also of some school groups and teams.'

'What do you think, Mark? Should we have copies of the ones of the two girls? If we are going to tackle Alex's friend, it might, if nothing else, prevent any denials.'

'Good idea. Do you know when the next term starts?'

'No, but I'll find out from Mrs Carlyle as soon as we've finished here. She's bound to know and while I'm at it, I'll check the timing for Matthew Travers's school as well. It might be best, too, if we go separately to the two places.'

'Any problems with letting us have copies of those photos, Reg?' Sinclair asked.

The man shook his head. 'You can have the ones I have here, sir. That might be the simplest arrangement and I can easily get further copies made if necessary by the people in the lab.'

'Excellent. I'll let you have a receipt for them. By the way, did you find any fingerprints on any of them apart from Lexie's?'

'There were on the camera, but not the photographs.'

'Interesting that. I wonder if the other girl was told that the camera wasn't working properly or not loaded. Otherwise, surely she would have wished to know how the pictures came out straight away so that Lexie could make further copies on her computer, if she wanted them.'

'Did you search any of the other rooms in the house, Reg?'

'Only the bathroom the girl used. Lavatory cisterns, particularly old fashioned types with them up near the ceiling, are popular sites for hiding drugs, but the one across the corridor is modern and at a low level. We did take away some packets of sweets including some Turkish delight from that drawer over there. They were dusted with a very fine powder, which proved to be sugar.'

'So you found no evidence that the girl was taking drugs of any sort?' Sarah asked.

'No, ma'am. We made a careful search of both this room and the bathroom and also checked the pockets of her anorak and coat, which were on hooks in the room in the hall adjacent to the downstairs toilet.'

'One last thing, Reg. We've seen from Dr Rawlings's photographs that the girl was wearing a wrist watch when she was killed. Did you find any documentation relating to it here?'

'No, sir, we didn't.'

'Any reason why the family shouldn't be allowed access to this room now?' Sarah asked.

'No, ma'am.'

Dr Hazel Mead came into the waiting room some fifteen minutes after the time of the two detectives' appointment with her. She was a slim, attractive woman, who appeared, Sarah thought, to be in her early thirties.

'Sorry to have kept you,' she said, when the introductions had been made. 'I deliberately made the appointment for thirty minutes after my last patient, but he happened to be a rather deaf old man, who just couldn't be hurried.'

'Don't worry,' Sarah said, 'it's very good of you to see us at such short notice. You've no doubt heard on the grapevine that, as the result of the 'flu epidemic, we've come down from London to head the inquiry into the death of Alex Travers.'

'Yes, Dr Rawlings's secretary did explain that to me when

she rang to make this appointment. May I suggest that we go along to my consulting room?'

She led them through the door at the end of the large waiting room, along the corridor and into a room with her name on the door and gestured towards the two chairs on the other side of her desk.

'Now, how may I help you?'

'We understand that you are the Travers's family doctor.'

The woman nodded. 'Yes and before you ask, you may be wondering why a very wealthy family should stick to the NHS, rather than going to a private practitioner. Well, I have never asked them that question, but it has always seemed to me that there are likely to have been several reasons. Firstly, none of the doctors here, myself included, do any private practice and I can also see the wisdom of Mr Travers having decided that there were Brownie points to be gained politically for making the same arrangements for medical care as the rest of the people in this very small country town.

'I have no doubt that you are particularly interested in why I prescribed contraception for Alex. Well, Mrs Carlyle, Mr Travers's mother-in-law, whom I know you have already met because she telephoned me after your visit to the house, was instrumental in advising young Alex to consult me about that question. I gather you know that she was brought back from the family's holiday in Corfu after having been discovered having sex with a young Greek boy out there. Mrs Carlyle was very direct about her concerns, saying that Alex was impulsive and physically extremely attractive and it was already quite clear that it was more than likely that she was going to continue to have sexual intercourse, whatever anybody said. After a long discussion, we both agreed that, provided that she wasn't pregnant already, it would be best if she was protected. She did not skate over likely difficulties with her parents and said that she was quite prepared to stand up and be counted if there was a row about it with her daughter and son-in-law. I gather that her daughter is the real stumbling block, having considered taking up Roman Catholicism and a pretty zealous section of it at that.

'I have to admit that I was not happy with becoming involved in a situation such as that, but after talking to a counsellor at my medical defence organization, I did get confirmation that I was within my rights to prescribe contraception under those circumstances without her parents' permission despite the girl still being just under sixteen.

'Luckily, one of my contemporaries at medical school runs a private family planning clinic in Oxford and I arranged for Alex to be seen there, Mrs Carlyle having agreed to settle the fees. The female doctor there organized a check for her with a veneriologist and when that was clear and after talking to the girl at length, agreed with my opinion that an Implanon would be the best option. It would have the double advantage of obviating the risk of the girl forgetting to take the Pill, or of it or any other form of contraceptive being found by her mother. An IUD is generally considered undesirable in girls of her age and she was not considered mature enough or sufficiently motivated to use a barrier device. Are you familiar with Implanons, Inspector?'

'I have heard of them,' Sarah said, 'and know that it is a form of contraceptive implant, as the name implies, but I don't know the details.'

'Yes, you're right, it is. It's about the same length as a matchstick, but very thin and it is put in the left arm in right handers about eight to ten centimetres above the elbow. It lasts about three years and can then easily be replaced. It takes very little time to fit and the procedure, using a local anaesthetic, is virtually painless. The incidence of side effects varies a great deal, but Alex was one of those who had no significant problems. Sometimes it is visible, but fortunately, considering the circumstances I have described, it was not so in her case.'

'So, the only non-medical people who know about this are Mrs Carlyle and the two of us.'

'Yes, unless the pathologist who did the post-mortem came across it.'

'He didn't say anything to us about it,' Sinclair said, 'and I think he would have done so, had he found it.'

'I can see what a difficult decision this must have been for you,' Sarah said.

'Indeed it was. The girl gave me the impression of being immature psychologically speaking, but certainly not physically. On top of that she was extremely pretty and, at least with me, came across as intelligent. However, from what her grandmother told me, emotionally she was all over the place, cyclothymic is what we call it.'

'Is it treatable?'

'Yes, but at that age one doesn't want to label someone with a psychiatric diagnosis, without giving the mood changes a chance to settle down spontaneously. After all, a degree of that sort of thing is common in adolescence. I was also proposing to keep a careful eye on her, having every confidence that Mrs Carlyle would let me know if things got out of hand.

'I saw Alex again during her half term break and again at the start of the summer holiday and everything was going well.'

'Have you any idea where Mr Travers stands with regard to all this?'

'No, but reading between the lines when I was talking to Mrs Carlyle, I got the impression that under the circumstances he might have had no problem with it, but I don't know whether she discussed it with him or not. There is no doubt at all in my mind that it is his wife who is the inflexible one in that marriage.'

'What did the girl say herself?'

'That no one apart from her grandmother, with whom she had discussed it at length, should know about it.'

The two detectives left the surgery deep in thought and sat in the car outside for a few minutes before driving off.

'What a difficult decision that must have been for Dr Mead,' Sinclair said. 'How do you think she would have been placed if the parents find out what she had prescribed?'

'I have come across this before and the legal situation is quite clear,' Sarah said. 'A doctor can prescribe contraception to a girl without the parents' knowledge or consent between the ages of fourteen and sixteen, provided they consider it essential for the girl's well being and that there is no question of her being coerced or exploited. Lexie was very nearly sixteen at the time she went to that clinic and we have no evidence to suggest that either coercion or exploitation was employed, nor that insufficient care was taken before making the decision. That is not to say that the family, and I would judge, particularly the girl's mother, would not have been very upset or worse had they known what arrangements had been made or if they found out now. All of which is potentially very tricky, particularly as the circumstances of her death strongly suggest a sexual motive.'

'I agree and I think it would be worth while discussing all this further with Rawlings and his wife. As it happens, I know that she has a medical qualification, although she hasn't practised for a number of years. It seems to me quite possible that he failed to find the implant and it might be a good idea to tell him about it and have a word with his wife at the same time. Why don't I ring him now and fix up a meeting with them both as soon as possible? I can tell him that we have some more interesting information on the case and would value his advice as well as his wife's view of the Travers family.'

'Should've invited you both to dinner, but I'm no sort of cook, as Henry has no doubt told you already, but I'm sure that a bottle from his wine cellar, of which he is so proud, and a few bits and pieces to eat will no doubt go down just as well if not better. By the way, I'm Helen.'

The amply built woman, who, Sinclair thought, must have weighed half as much again as the spare forensic pathologist, gave them both a bone crunching handshake and after Sinclair had introduced himself and Sarah, she strode towards the staircase which rose from the hall.

'Henry!' she bellowed, 'they're here.'

The forensic pathologist appeared at the head of the stairs seconds later. 'Splendid,' he said. 'Punctual as ever, I see. You're both very welcome. Won't be a minute. Helen, perhaps you'd show them into the drawing room.'

'That terrible man is always banging on about how unpunctual young people are these days, but I see that you've got his number,' the woman said after they were sitting down. 'He was clock watching just now as always and went upstairs to do something or other after pacing about in the hall a good five minutes before you arrived, muttering something about knowing you would be late. Your arrival on the dot has made my day, I can tell you. Speak of the devil!'

Sinclair got to his feet as Rawlings came into the room carrying a large silver tray on which was a bottle of wine and four elaborately cut glasses. He set it down on the circular table, on which were already plates of nuts and savoury biscuits, which had been garnished with slices of cheese, smoked salmon and pâté, and there was also a bowl of fruit.

'You wanted to know about the Travers family?' Rawlings said, when he had finished serving the wine and had handed round the biscuits.

'Yes,' Sinclair said. 'We have met the dead girl's parents, her grandmother and her brother, as well as the gardener and his assistant, but only at a superficial level so far. The only one of the family we have left out up to now is the younger daughter, Lizzie and we'd welcome any views you have about any of them.'

'As I said earlier, Helen knows more about them than I do. Helen!'

The woman gave the two detectives a wry smile. 'If I don't get down to the nitty-gritty straight away, I'll never hear the last of it,' the woman said, raising her eyebrows in her husband's direction. 'The Traverses arrival here, some twelve years ago, caused something of a stir as the big house had been empty for so long and the previous incumbent was virtually a recluse. This is also a quiet sort of place and there were fears that the estate might be invaded by noisy nouveaux riches, or turned into a bed and breakfast, or, even worse, pulled down and a hotel built on the site. The previous family there had been beset by tragedy. The Forrests' two sons were both killed while serving with the RAF in the war. The house was requisitioned at that time and was used as a military convalescent home and Mr and Mrs Forrest moved into a small house in the village. After the war, they did go back to the big house, were awarded some compensation for the damage caused and did make an attempt to refurbish it. I'm sure I don't need to tell you that times remained very difficult for a number of years after the war and it proved too much for Mr Forrest, who, in any case wasn't in the best of health, and he died in the early 1950s. His wife became, as I said, a virtual recluse and lived on the ground floor, being looked after by the housekeeper, who had been with them throughout the war and was too old to be called up.

'When the old lady died some twelve years ago, the house remained unoccupied for some time and was then bought by Richard Travers. I don't know where all the money came from, but the house was modernized and the grounds restyled with the addition of a swimming pool next to an area which became a tennis court. He moved in some ten years or so ago with his wife, son and newly adopted daughter, Lexie, the poor girl who was killed so recently. Not long after they did so, they had another child, a girl who must be about seven or eight years old by now and Mrs Carlyle, Travers's mother-in-law, who had just been widowed, also came to live with them at much the same time.

'In many ways, the family's arrival proved to be an excellent thing for the village. The incumbent Tory MP had died not long before the family's arrival and Richard, who had already been an unsuccessful candidate elsewhere at the previous election, won this seat, which is presumably why they came to live here. He has been like a breath of fresh air, being energetic, personable and full of ideas for the neighbourhood and particularly the village. I have to say that the fact that his wife is very high church and recently has been rumoured to be flirting with a move to Rome, has not gone down well and has created some problems with the organizers of the traditional C of E activities here. What really saved the day, though, was the arrival of Mrs Carlyle, Mrs Travers's mother. She is a live wire, and although clearly not interested in religion in any shape or form, has thrown herself into all other aspects of village life both enthusiastically and effectively.'

Mrs Rawlings looked across at her husband with a wry smile on her face. 'I know what Henry is thinking and that is "get on with it, woman", however, I thought that some background information would be important. Now, how about the dead girl? Firstly, you must be thinking, what does an elderly woman in her late sixties – yes, I am several years older than Henry – know about adolescent girls? The answer is quite a lot as we have two daughters and a son, as well as five grandchildren. The one I would like to tell you about is Rebecca, the youngest grandchild, because, in some ways, she is rather like Alex was and is much the same age. She is also outgoing, pretty and cheerful, but there is one very big difference. She understands already that there are limits and, how shall I put it, times when restraint is important. Let me give you an example. Over the last couple of years, both girls have helped me with the stall I run at the village fête. Not surprisingly, Rebecca, probably advised by her mother, always dresses down for the event, with her hemline, not so long as to look dowdy, but long enough not to upset the old biddies, who are my main customers. She is patient with them and doesn't get cross if they can't make up their minds, something which is par for the course.

'Lexie was quite different. Her dresses were usually half way up her thighs, she was braless under her tops and that wasn't exactly good for business with my usual clientele of elderly women. If an old trot was dithering over the choice between plum or raspberry jam, she would say cheerfully: "Why not have both for the price of one?" Her presence also resulted in the arrival of boys and young and not so young men, wanting to stare at the goods that were only too visible under her very thin shirts.

'Why, you might ask, hadn't her mother or grandmother done something about it right from the beginning? Well, as to the mother, Mrs Travers, she is one of those managerial types, absolutely clear in her own mind that her way of doing things is the right one and dismissive of any hint of criticism – I also heard on the grapevine that she had rather given up on Lexie and left her management largely to her mother and husband. Mrs Carlyle is a very different sort of person and I did decide recently to have a chat with her about Lexie. She was, as I had hoped, not the least dismissive or combative about my concerns. She told me that she was as worried about Lexie as I obviously was, but that she was in a very difficult position. It was no secret, she said, that she didn't go along with her daughter's religious views and she also believed that Madeleine had rather given up on Lexie. She told me that her daughter was prudish in the extreme and had heard her say that she believed the Devil to be inside the girl. Mrs Carlyle said that she had already spoken to the girl about the way she dressed at village activities and had threatened to tell her father about it unless she showed more restraint.'

'Did that work?' Sarah asked.

'After a style, but I had no confidence that it would last.'

'Had her mother given up on her completely by then?' Sinclair said.

Helen Rawlings looked in his direction. 'Henry has often told me what a film buff, you are, Mr Sinclair, and I'm sure that you must either have seen or heard about Roman Polanski's film, *Rosemary's Baby.'* The woman glanced across at Sarah. 'You look puzzled, my dear; perhaps I should explain. The film dates from the late sixties and is about a young couple who move into an apartment in New York next to a couple who turn out to be Satanists. Rosemary has a nightmare in which she is ravished by the Devil and soon after she discovers that she is pregnant and when the baby is born she is told that he has died. She hears a baby crying in the adjacent flat, goes through a communicating door and sees the baby's strange, staring eyes. One is left, at one end of the scale, not believing in the concept of the Devil and that the woman is deluded and suffering from depression, but on the other, having the uneasy feeling that there might have been diabolic intervention in that instance.

'At any minute, my husband will say that we've had quite enough of this Gothic horror stuff. He's probably right, but nevertheless I thought it would illustrate just how far Madeleine Travers had gone in believing that poor Lexie was possessed, if not by the Devil, by evil spirits. As for me, I am convinced that there was something wrong with the girl other than just a hereditary predisposition to emotional instability and promiscuity. I don't know enough about mental illness in adolescents to be able to hazard a guess as to the cause, particularly as no one seems to know anything about her natural parents, but in the days when

I was practising medicine, I never came across a girl like her.

'Mrs Carlyle did speak to me about Alex on a number of occasions, knowing that I had a medical qualification, and she didn't exactly hold back over details of Lexie's behaviour, notably in Corfu, but she did ask me not to broadcast what we had been discussing nor her opinions about her daughter.'

'How did you respond to that?' Sarah asked.

The woman smiled. 'With an indeterminate nod. Need I say I don't consider what I have been doing just now could be construed as broadcasting.'

Rawlings let out a loud guffaw. 'You won't get any change out of her, my dear Miss Prescott, believe you me.'

Sarah smiled and turned back towards the woman. 'How did Mr Travers get on with Lexie?'

'I have seen the two of them together on a number of occasions and they seemed very relaxed with one another. To give you an example, he cheered her on when she entered the sack race at the village fête and when she won, he was obviously delighted and gave her a hug. It's very difficult to fake genuine love and enthusiasm and I'm quite convinced that he wasn't doing so.'

'How about Phil Carter, the young fellow who found the girl's body?' Sinclair said. 'Do you know anything about him, Mrs Rawlings? I gather that he is a local lad.'

'Have you met him?'

'Yes, we have.'

'Well, you'll know that he's self effacing and diffident, but he's very polite and a nice fellow. He's helped me a few times with setting up my tent and stall at the fair. His mother is nice enough, but his father is a bully and too many pints most evenings at the pub don't help, either.'

'Mrs Carlyle implied that Phil was more than a bit interested in Alex,' Sarah said, 'but told me that she thought it unlikely that they were having full sex together and that she was just teasing him in that way. In fact, there is no doubt at all that she was wrong and that they had done so, even though it seems to have been on one occasion only.'

'I'm sorry to hear about that and I hope that it doesn't get around. I have already told you about Phil's father and I've also seen the bruises on his downtrodden mother's arms when she's been helping with the tea stall and I shudder to think what he would do to the poor boy if he were to find out. There are also rumours that Fred Palmer, the gardener, fancies Phil. It's a hotbed of gossip, this place, and Fred comes in for more than his fair share. He lives in a house on the edge of the village. His parents died before we came down here, but I gather that his father was a bee-keeper and they had a bit of a cottage industry making honey, which apparently was pretty successful. Evidently, Palmer has lived alone in the house ever since their deaths, long before we came down here.'

'But he didn't keep up the honey production?'

'No, and all I know about him is that he worked as a gardener and general handyman for Mrs Forrest and then the Traverses took him on.'

'Is he popular in the village.'

'No, he isn't. Being a bit grumpy and a solitary, antisocial sort of fellow, unmarried and thought never to have had a woman in his life, there have been rumours about him, in particular that he might be gay. One of the men was unwise enough to be having a laugh about that in the pub and made a remark about him being a "shirtlifter". He wasn't to know that Fred had just come in and he got decked as a result. He's a powerful man is Fred and the story may well be true. Personally, I don't get those vibes from him myself. I don't believe he's that way inclined and is just one of those who's never felt Cupid's darts. Anyway, I rather like him in his rough and ready way. He really knows his horticultural stuff, he's an excellent gardener and often wins prizes for his vegetables at the local fruit and flower show and his photographs of flowers, in particular, are brilliant. He also turns his hand to all sort of things in the house. If a tap is dripping, a drain blocked or a puncture in one of the children's bikes, he'll fix it. Mrs Carlyle won't have a word said against him.'

'Well, thank you for all that background, Mrs Rawlings, that was extremely helpful.'

'Think nothing of it. If I can be of any further assistance, you only have to ask.'

*

'I saw you having an aside with Rawlings just before we left,' Sarah said when the two of them were driving back to Mrs Sinclair's house. 'Did you tell him about the Implanon?'

'Yes, I had a quiet word with him just before we left and I was very impressed by his response. He admitted that he had missed it, thanked me for the tip and said that he would look for it. Anyway, what did you make of all that we've discovered so far?'

'Well, Mrs Carlyle, without being too direct about it, implied to me that her daughter had no idea how to handle a difficult adolescent girl and that there was nothing more wrong with Alex other than that. Travers, himself, was obviously using his parliamentary skills to be as non-committal as possible, while his wife almost seemed to believe that even possession by the Devil was involved. Oh, and finally, Mrs Rawlings clearly felt that the girl was more than just a difficult adolescent and that she might have had a psychiatric or even physical disorder.'

'I agree with all that and inevitably one wonders if Rawlings himself suspects the same thing, although he clearly found nothing significant at the post mortem apart from her physical injuries. I think that the next ports of call should be the two schools. The logical choice would be for you to handle the girls' side and for me to go to the other.'

Sarah nodded. 'That makes sense. However, it has to be

said that I have virtually no experience at all of girls' boarding schools and the one I did visit on a case was a Catholic one and the mother superior frightened the daylights out of me. I think it would be a good idea to give the school a ring rather than just turning up. Perhaps I'll do the same with Rosie Maxwell's parents before they go off to work in the hope of dropping in to see them on the way, even if it means making a very early start. Ideally, I think it would be best for me to see them first.'

'Good idea. I'll do the same with Matthew's school and in the interests of keeping Travers on side, I'll also give him a call directly we get back to my mother's house to tell him what we are proposing to do.'

FIVE

WHEN SINCLAIR ARRIVED at Crichton College, he spoke to the porter at the gatehouse by the side of the entrance to the grounds and was directed to the office in the building at the end of the drive.

The middle-aged woman who had been sitting behind the desk got to her feet when he went in.

'My name's Margaret Stone,' she said, shaking him by the hand. 'I'm the head administrator's secretary. And you must be Mr Sinclair. I know you were expecting to meet the head-master,' she continued when they were sitting down, 'but he was called to a meeting with the chairman of the board early this morning and asked me to give you his apologies. Dr Fisher, one of the housemasters and the deputy head, will be seeing you instead.'

Sinclair was intrigued by the fact that the woman obviously didn't know that he was a policeman or the reason he had come to the school, and why that was so became clear when one of the porters showed him across a large court-yard, through an arch and up a stone staircase to the study on the first floor.

'Good to see you, Sinclair,' the slightly built man, who was wearing glasses and looked to be in his early forties, said, when he had got out of his chair behind the desk, walked across the room and shaken the detective's hand. 'My name is Gerald Fisher. I'm Matthew's housemaster and in view of what you told the Head on the telephone, he thought it best if your visit wasn't made obvious to all and sundry, the boy being in rather a fragile state. That's why I'm seeing you here rather than in the house itself. He also agreed with your opinion that it would be better not to upset the young man in advance. I propose to fetch him when the class he is attending finishes, which should be in about ten minutes and fortunately he has a free period after that, so you will be able to take your time.'

'That sounds excellent. My colleague and I have already spoken to Matthew's parents and I met the young man very briefly on his own, shortly before he returned here for the start of term. I would be very interested to hear how he has settled in, the tragedy of his sister's death being so recent.'

The man put his fingertips together and thought for a few moments before replying. 'I have been very concerned about Matthew for some time. You may not know that the College was founded by Bishop Franklin in the 1840s and religion and regular chapel attendance are very important parts of our ethos here, but one has to admit that neither are by any means shared by all and that includes some of the staff.

Adolescence is a time when children are very impressionable and I believe that some space is required for many of
them at that time in a number of different directions. You
see, while the majority of the boys here get along well
enough with a middle way, there are some who become
virtually obsessed with concepts of sin and unworthiness,
often related to sexual matters of one sort or another, while
others are the complete opposite and have no interest in
religion at all, at best finding it incomprehensible and at
worst a mockery.'

'And Matthew is one of those in the second category?'

'Yes, he is. Quite a few of the boys here find it very difficult to cope with adolescence and the associated rapid
changes in their bodies and the hormonal surges. In my
view, attributing sexual thoughts and urges to sin is a
serious mistake, particularly with boys, like Matthew, who
are both obsessional and introspective. It's quite possible, I
believe, that he also has aggressive instincts that he does
everything possible to hide. I say that because you only
have to see him on the rugby pitch and in the boxing ring
when at times, restraint goes out of the window.

'I am sorry to have to say that his particular problems
have not been helped, indeed they have been aggravated, by
the influence brought to bear on him by the appointment,
some two years ago, of the assistant chaplain, one Ian
Hughes. He is a young man. Inevitably his experience of life
in general and adolescent boys in particular cannot have

been great and I gather that he takes a very fundamental view of religion and the sinfulness of sexual thoughts and urges outside of a Christian marriage. Such views are very much at odds with the traditions and ethos of this school and I have been seriously considering discussing the matter with the Head, not least because Matthew has been spending even more time with Hughes since his return here at the beginning of this term.'

'Is the headmaster already aware of your recent concerns about Matthew?'

'Not so far, but I have been thinking first of having a face to face chat about Matthew with his father, who, as you may not know, was at school here himself, as was his grandfather.'

'Have you met Mr Travers before?'

'Yes, on a couple of occasions at Speech Days and I got a very favourable impression of him. I am, of course, well aware that he is an MP and the tragedy of his daughter's death must have been particularly hard for him as I'm quite sure that the press will have already latched on to it.'

'What is your view of the usefulness of my talking to Mr Hughes about Matthew on his own?'

'To be brutally frank, I think you would be wasting your time.'

'Have you spoken to Matthew in detail yourself since his return here?'

'I have tried, but I wasn't able to get any response from

him and have to say that I think it unlikely that he will react to you any differently.'

'I see. Nonetheless, I would like to see Matthew, and as we've already met briefly, it's not as if I will be a complete stranger to him. I have no objection to Hughes being present on this occasion and I would appreciate if you were here, too.'

'Luckily, as I told you, Matthew has a free period next, but I think it would be undesirable for him to be late for or miss the last class before lunch. I'm sure you know what boys are like and if he doesn't turn up the rumour mongers will no doubt get into their stride, particularly if they discover that you have been talking to him and that you are a policeman.'

'Don't worry, I quite understand. Anyway, I didn't have it in mind to spend all that long with him and there's no danger of his missing his next lesson.'

Matthew Travers looked terrible, Sinclair thought, when he came into the room accompanied by the assistant chaplain. There was little colour in his cheeks and beads of sweat were standing out on his forehead. After shaking the young man by the hand the detective introduced himself to the austere looking man, who accompanied him. He didn't look to be more than in his late twenties and, like Matthew, was deathly pale and in addition was painfully thin, such that his cheekbones stood out.

'Do sit down, Matthew, and you, Mr Hughes.'

The assistant chaplain remained standing where he was, stared at Sinclair for a few moments and then said: 'I object strongly to this young man being taken out of school and subjected to an inquisition.'

Sinclair met his gaze until the silence became uncomfortable, then got to his feet and said: 'If you would excuse us for a moment, Mr Fisher and you, Matthew, I would like a quick word with Mr Hughes outside.'

He made a gesture towards the door and then opened it, waiting by its side, until, very slowly, the man walked towards it. After he had gone out into the corridor, Sinclair closed the door almost soundlessly and with his back to it, looked at the man straight in the eye, and said:

'Recently, Matthew Travers's sister, a sixteen-year-old girl, was physically assaulted and died as the result of it. I have come here to speak to him about her with the agreement of the headmaster and with the express knowledge of his father and grandfather, both of whom are prominent and influential people in the community, not to mention former pupils of this school.

'The whole family is in the process of being interviewed as the result of her violent death and Matthew has not been singled out, nor have I any intention of either bullying him or, as you put it, submitting him to an inquisition. I would also point out that he has not been taken out of school. At worst he has had to forfeit his free period. Your opening comment was completely unjustified and out of place and furthermore, I should warn you that obstructing the police in the course of their legitimate inquiries is an offence and you would do well to bear that in mind.

'Now, is that quite clear? There is no need for either the Headmaster, or the Travers family to hear about your attitude or what you said just now, but a condition of your coming back into that room is your assurance that there will be no further comments or interruptions of that nature.'

The chaplain stared at the detective for a moment or two. 'Very well, but I am not going to abandon the young man in his hour of need.'

'I am not asking you to do that, but you should bear in mind what I have just said.'

Sinclair went back to the door, reopened it and made a gesture with his hand towards the empty chair next to that of the housemaster. He then turned towards Matthew Travers, smiling at him.

'My apologies for that interruption. I won't keep you long, Matthew, and you will be in plenty of time for your next class. Now, I imagine that you saw Alex early on the morning that she died, perhaps at breakfast. Did she seem in any way different then?'

There was a short pause. 'No, sir. My father usually reads the paper at breakfast, but that morning he had already left the house early to go to a meeting at the Houses of

Parliament. Normally, none of us ever says much at breakfast as my father likes to study the paper in reasonable
quiet and none of us likes to upset him. That morning,
though, Alex and Elizabeth were arguing noisily with one
another.'

'What about?'

'That's what made it so irritating. I wasn't feeling very
well that morning, having a bit of a stomach upset, and the
two girls were squabbling. It was so stupid, with Lizzie
saying that Alex was trying to take more than her fair share
of the fruit salad that we usually have with our cereal,
which I wasn't able to face. They would never have done so
if my father had been there and I think that annoyed my
mother more than anything else as she likes to be in charge
of everything. She was really cross, leaned across the table
to take the bowl of fruit salad from Alex and managed to
knock the milk jug over, breaking it. She then told Alex that
it was all her fault and sent her up to her room at once
without allowing her to finish her breakfast. She followed
Alex out and I could hear her shouting at her, but not
exactly what she said. Anyway, my mother came back a few
minutes later, red in the face and clearly very angry and
upset. I could only think that Alex must have said something really bad to her. Anyway, I can't stand scenes like
that and when my mother told me to get a cloth, Mrs
Weston, the housekeeper, saw that I was looking unwell and
told me not to worry, saying that she would deal with the

problem in the breakfast room. I didn't go back there myself, being worried that I might be sick and went into the downstairs cloakroom and later up to my room when I felt a bit better.'

'Did Alex get on your mother's nerves a lot?'

'She certainly did. As I said, my mother likes to feel that she is in control of everybody and the fact that both my father and grandmother could obviously cope with Alex's moods much better than her, really annoyed her.'

'How did they manage to deal with her?'

'By realizing that her outbursts never lasted long and that a quiet word with her when she had settled down almost always did the trick.'

'And what about you?'

'Like my father, I don't like rows, nor do I like to say much at breakfast as I am usually thinking about what I am going to do during the day. That morning, I was planning to complete the holiday task I had been set by my form master, but I didn't go up to my room straight away. As I told you, I was feeling so unwell that I went into the downstairs cloakroom as I was frightened that I might be sick on the stairs or something like that. Anyway, after quite some time, it must have been at least half an hour, I went up to my room and lay down for a bit. I must have fallen asleep, because when I looked at my clock I saw that it was just after ten. Feeling a lot better, I washed my face and hands and decided to go out into the garden for a bit to get some fresh air.'

125

'Did you see anybody out there?'

'My sister Lizzie was on the swing and I pushed her for a bit as she wanted to go really high and then I walked with her back to the house after she had got off and had shown me the fuchsia in her small garden plot. She was going to put it in a nice pot and give to our grandma for her seventieth birthday, which is coming up shortly.'

'Was anyone else there?'

'Just Palmer, the gardener, who was working nearby. After a few minutes, I went back to my room and was working on my holiday task when I heard banging on the terrace door. I went out on to the landing and saw my grandmother talking to someone in the hall down there. I remember that I called down and asked what was happening.'

'And what did she say?'

'Just that there was nothing to worry about and that she would deal with it. I went back into my room and not long after heard the ambulance and police cars arriving. That was when I was told what had happened to Alex and that upset me so much that I wasn't able to settle down or concentrate on any work during the rest of the time I was at home before term started. You will remember seeing me, sir, when I was trying to get my mind off what had happened by practising my golf at the net. It was a relief to get back to school here.'

'Did you go outside the house at all between breakfast

and starting your work apart from when you saw Lizzie and looked at her plant?'

'No, sir.'

'Well, thank you, Matthew. That's all I need from you for the time being, but I may need to see you again later, depending how our investigation proceeds.'

Sinclair got to his feet and watched as Matthew Travers and the chaplain walked out of the door, neither of them looking back or saying anything.

'I see what you meant about that fellow,' Sinclair said, when the sound of the footsteps receded and then became inaudible.

Mr Fisher shook his head. 'Hughes's remark when he came in here vis-à-vis your arrival was quite out of order and I will not stand for it. I have been concerned about him for some time. I haven't had all that much to do with him, but another member of staff told me that he seems to have an obsession about mortification of the flesh being necessary to purge boys of their sins. He thinks that the banning of corporal punishment in schools is largely responsible for the moral collapse of the youth of today. I will be speaking to the Head about the situation as a whole and Hughes's behaviour just now in particular, as soon as he returns. We may also decide that it is in Matthew's interest to have some time away from school. No doubt, though, before taking such a step I'm sure the Head will be looking to have a face to face discussion with Mr Travers.'

'I'm very grateful to you for your help, Mr Fisher,' Sinclair said. 'It has been very important for me to assess Matthew's state of mind and I will let you know if I need to see him again. In the meantime, I am very reassured that you will be keeping a careful eye on him and consulting the headmaster about the relationship between him and Hughes.'

Sarah telephoned Craven Park School soon after nine o'clock that morning and managed to arrange an appointment with the headmistress, Barbara Elliott, for eleven o'clock. The school was situated some thirty miles from Oxford and was in spacious grounds on the edge of a village.

'I have spoken at length to Alex Travers's parents and also telephoned those of Rosemary Maxwell earlier this morning, arranging to see them briefly on my way here before they went to work,' Sarah said when she had introduced herself. 'They were quite happy for me to talk to their daughter on her own and I have Mr Maxwell's office phone number should you require confirmation.'

Barbara Elliott gave her a wintry smile. 'That won't be necessary, Inspector. Mr Maxwell has already telephoned me. Earlier, I also had a long face to face conversation with Sir Michael Travers, Alexandra's grandfather, who, as I'm sure you know already, is the Chairman of our Board of Governors, about the tragedy of Alexandra's death and I assure you that you will have my full cooperation.

'You would also, no doubt, like to talk to Mary Lake, who

is in charge of Alexandra's and Rosemary's house and there will be no problem about that, either.'

'Will I also be able to see the young woman who found the two girls in the shower?'

'May I ask who told you about that incident?'

'It was Alex's father, but he didn't go into any great detail.'

'I see. Well no, that won't be possible, at least not here. You see, during my initial interview with the young woman, Alison Carter, I made it quite clear that in matters of discipline in the boarding house and any problem she might have should be reported to the housemistress, in that case, Miss Lake. When she came direct to me after that incident in the shower, I was forced to look into it and inevitably I also had to mention it to Sir Michael, as his granddaughter was involved. We interviewed the student teacher and the two girls and concluded that Miss Carter was making a mountain out of a molehill, but nevertheless that the girls should be warned about their future behaviour. They also had some privileges withdrawn for the rest of term. We were both convinced that the student teacher had over-reacted and I felt it would be in her best interests to leave here early.'

'I see.'

'Whom do you wish to see first?'

'Miss Lake, if that is convenient for her. I would like to get an idea of Alexandra as a person and any other problems there might have been with her in the house. After that, I might be in a better position to tackle her friend, Rosemary. After that, I thought I might call on Sir Michael at his house on my way back, rather than just telephoning him, as we have not met yet. I gather that he lives not far from here. Perhaps I might be permitted to telephone him from here when I have finished talking to Rosemary.'

'Of course, but before you do all that, it might be helpful if I were to give you a thumbnail sketch of the history of this school. The original purpose, as set out by Lady Craven, the widow of Sir Henry, was to provide education for girls on the lines pioneered at the North London Collegiate School and Cheltenham Ladies College, which were founded by the redoubtable Misses Buss and Beale in the 1850s. Their hope was that women would eventually be allowed to sit for university degrees and at long last become the academic equals of men. Lady Craven was a great supporter of that ideal. When her husband died and as there were no heirs, she decided to donate the house and grounds, together with a large endowment, so that a girls' boarding school should be set up. A Board of Governors was appointed, buildings, incorporating the original house, constructed and the school opened in 1896. It flourished and unlike the boys' public schools, like Marlborough and Cheltenham, neither of which are that far from here, and which have become co-educational, it has remained single sex.'

'Thank you, that was both most interesting and helpful.'

*

Margaret Lake had a warm and friendly manner, which was apparent from the moment that Sarah introduced herself and had shaken her hand.

'Miss Elliott has already explained about your visit,' she said. 'How may I help you?'

'We are still at the stage of trying to find out as much as possible about Alexandra from those who knew her well here. I had in mind any comments you might have about her behaviour, her academic ability, her personality, her friends – that type of thing.'

'For what it's worth I think there was something seriously wrong with the girl.'

'In what way?'

'Let me explain, but first perhaps I should say a little about this school. By its very nature, the girls here are a very select group. Academically, the entrance standards are high. I have been here for over ten years now and before that, worked in a state comprehensive school and I like to think that I know a good deal about adolescent girls, particularly since I became a house mistress here. There is a strong Church of England ethos at the school and attendance at chapel each morning and on Sundays is obligatory. Music is also an important part of the curriculum, as is sport. The fees are high, although quite a few scholarships are available. The aim is to prepare girls for life and in particular higher education at university and music and regular organized games are very much part of the curriculum.

'Discipline has always been tight here and still is and that suits the majority of the girls here very well, although for some it is an ordeal and a few are very unhappy and manage to persuade their parents to take them away.

'Now, as regards Alexandra, perhaps I shouldn't have used the word "wrong", but it seemed to me that the girl's emotions were never completely under control and that coloured everything she did.'

'In what way?'

'It was a roller coaster ride as far as dealing with her was concerned. At times she was bubbling with energy and *joie de vivre* and at others in the depths of despair, all for no obvious reason. Then there were her sexual impulses, which at times were completely out of control.'

'How exactly?'

'Occasionally, she would be sitting in class and I could see her getting progressively more restless and then she would stiffen, go red in the face and gradually relax. Sooner or later, the same thing would happen again.' The woman smiled. 'I know I must sound insufferably coy in the way I've put it, but that comes from working in an environment like this.'

'Don't worry,' Sarah said. 'I know exactly what you're talking about. I gathered from her mother and grandmother that she was also highly emotional in other ways, too.'

'Yes, that's true. Many adolescent girls are a bit like that, but never, in my experience, to that extent.'

'How about temper? Did she ever lack restraint in that way as well?'

'Surprisingly, perhaps, she didn't and certainly had no malice in her. The other girls were sometimes frightened by her total lack of inhibition, but that was, I think, due to the fact such a thing was totally alien to the culture here. Extravagant displays of anything are strongly discouraged and the girls are expected to be demure, hard working, modest and obedient. I can't imagine what Alex was like with boys. I say that because some of her behaviour here, which really amounted to exhibitionism, was also over the top. Wandering around her dormitory with just a towel round her middle and sometimes not even that, when she would take it off and flick it at passing girls' bottoms, was, as you may imagine, hardly the sort of thing to be tolerated by most of the extravagantly modest and prim girls here.

'Anyway, what precipitated the final drama was that she and Rosemary Maxwell were discovered sharing a shower. Unfortunately, the person who did the discovering was a very buttoned up young woman, one Alison Carter, who had been seconded here for a term from her teacher training college, for teaching practice. The two girls were making quite a lot of noise, but with the glass doors of the cubicle being steamed up in the room, she obviously wouldn't have been able to see anything clearly, which was probably just as well as she is a very innocent young woman and had she taken in what was really going on, the shock to her system might have been too much for her. Anyway, she concluded that the two girls were behaving in a disgraceful fashion, as she put it when reporting the matter to the headmistress, and she went as far as to say that both of them should be expelled.

'Miss Elliot cut her short and reminded her that she had already been told that any disciplinary matters should be discussed with the appropriate housemistress first and that she should see me about it immediately.

'After I had seen the young woman myself, interviewed the two girls and discussed it with the head, we decided that the evidence was by no means clear and that the student had exceeded her terms of reference. Miss Elliott told me to have a serious talk to the two girls and warn them that repeat of any further behaviour like that would result in their expulsion.'

'And presumably you did so?'

'Yes I did and saw them individually. I told each of them that only they knew what they were, in fact, doing, but that in my view they had been lucky not to have been expelled and that there was to be no repeat of anything of that sort again. I got tears from Rosemary and as for Alex, she just about managed to hide a grin. All that was in the middle of last term and I have to say that there was no further trouble and even Alex seemed to have calmed down a bit, perhaps because Rosemary was kept away from her. A great help was that Sir Michael Travers, who knew Rosemary quite well, having had her to stay with Alex at his house on a couple of occasions, had a word with both girls as well. He is a very soft spoken man, but has a remarkable way with him and he definitely made a deep impression on both girls.'

'What sort of girl is Rosemary?'

'Easily led would, I think, be the best way of putting it. She was rather lonely when she first came here, but once Alex took her up, she changed considerably, developing confidence in herself. Had it not been for Alex, I'm quite sure that she would never have got up to high jinks with anyone, let alone in the shower.'

'And how has she taken the news of Alex's death?'

'Not at all badly, all things considered. Directly I heard the sad news, I telephoned her parents. Naturally, I was wondering how she was taking it and whether it was wise for her to come back here for the start of this term, which was only a short time after the tragedy had occurred. They were quite clear in their minds that that would be the best thing for her, having already discussed it with the girl. They were quite right. She was very quiet and withdrawn to start with, but the others in the house have rallied round and she has settled back in pretty well.'

'As I explained, I will need to have a chat to Rosemary. Is there anywhere quiet, well away from the other girls, where I might see her?'

'I have a class to take now so you're very welcome to use this study if you like. I expect you'll have gone by the time I get back, and I do hope that you catch the monster who did this terrible thing. Alex's death has upset me a very great deal. She was such a lovely girl and so much fun when she was not out of control and it was always my hope that in time she would mature and settle down.'

Sarah was sitting behind the housemistress's desk, when she heard the soft knock on the door. She went across to open it herself, giving the anxious-looking girl, who was standing outside, a smile.

'Hello,' she said, 'my name is Sarah Prescott, Inspector Prescott, and, as Miss Lake must have told you, my colleague and I have come down from London to look into the sad business of Alex's death. You must be Rosemary. I know that you were her special friend, which is why I wanted to have a word with you. Why don't you sit here?'

Rather than using the housemistress's chair behind the desk, Sarah pulled up another one which had been resting against the wall and positioned it directly opposite, but not too close to the girl.

'I saw your parents briefly earlier today and explained that as you were Alex's closest friend here, I wanted to have a word with you about her and they were quite happy about that, as was your housemistress, Miss Lake, whom I have just seen. I have been told about the shower episode, but not the whole truth about that, nor about the photographs we found on Lexie's camera.'

All the colour went out of the girl's face. 'Oh, my God, not the ones I thought we were pretending to take down by the pool? Lexie told me that there wasn't a card in the camera and that it would just be a bit of pretend fun.'

'We guessed that that was what might have happened. We found the camera in Lexie's room and have already seen the images on it, but I see no reason why anyone other than my colleague and I should do so. Why not tell me exactly how they came to be taken and what really happened in the shower?'

'You're quite sure that no one else knows about those pictures?'

'Yes, I am. The camera was hidden in Lexie's room and the only fingerprints on them were hers and one other set which presumably are yours.'

There was a long pause, while the girl sat there biting her lip and then she gave an almost imperceptible nod.

'We had been sunbathing in the clearing down by the pond at the bottom of the garden at Lexie's house, when she suddenly said: "I'm bored, why don't we pretend to take some glamour shots." "Why pretend?" I asked. "My camera's on the blink," she replied and then said: "You go first."

'There wasn't too much to it to start with, then she dared me to take the top of my bikini off, then the bottom part as well. After that she did a turn herself in much the same way, but then stuck her tongue out at me and said: "Now for the porn shots."

'If the pictures really did come out, you'll know what I mean. I didn't want to follow what she had done, but you didn't know Lexie, did you? Well, it was very difficult to say no to her when she was on a high like she was that day. She called me a chicken and told me she'd give me a reward if I did the same.'

'I have some idea of what that might have been.'

The girl nodded, a tear slowly trickling down her cheek. 'Please don't make me tell you exactly what it was.'

'Don't worry, I've come across this sort of thing in my job before and you've no need to spell it out. As for Lexie, I already have a very clear idea of exactly what she was capable of getting up to. Now what about that shower?'

'That soppy woman, Miss Carter, heard us from out in the corridor making rather a lot of noise, came in and opened the door of the shower. Lexie told me not to worry as she was quite sure that she would never be able to bring herself to tell Miss Lake what we were actually doing and we should say that we were just washing each other's hair and having a giggle about it. I was terrified because I didn't think for one moment that it would work, particularly if the Head got to hear about it, as she was bound to do with Miss Carter only being a student teacher. I also knew that Miss Lake wouldn't be taken in, either, and I really thought that we were going to be expelled.

'I hate it here and I wouldn't have minded having to leave, but my parents aren't all that well off, not like the Traverses, and I know it's a struggle for them and they've had to do without nice holidays and other things as well in order to send me here. So you see I knew how upset and disappointed they would be and I couldn't do that to them.'

'Was Lexie as worried as you?'

'No, she laughed the whole thing off, saying that her granddad, who was chairman of the board of governors, would fix things.'

'Yes, I've already heard about that from Miss Lake. Do you know Mr Travers, senior, yourself?'

'Lexie used to go to his house for lunch on Sundays some-times and on a couple of occasions I was asked as well and also stayed with her there twice. He's ever such a nice man and since his wife died, he's been looked after by his house-keeper.'

'Did Lexie like going there?'

'Oh, yes. It's funny because when I stayed with her at her home, I found it really uncomfortable because she could be so rude to her mother and the only people she really seemed to like were her grandma and her father, and he was hardly ever there. I remember she said once that her grandma and granddad ought to get together and then she might be able to live with them.'

'How did Lexie get on with her young sister?'

'Quite well, but she often found her a bit much, as Lizzie

was always wanting her to play with her. Her granddad's housekeeper has her daughter living with her in the house, a girl of about the same age as us, but Wendy has Down's Syndrome. Lexie was very sweet with her, never getting impatient with her as she so often did with Lizzie and me.'

'Did Lexie say what her granddad had to say to her about that shower business?'

'It wasn't only to her, he spoke to the two of us together at the school. We were really embarrassed because he was so nice about it. He said he understood why we found the school oppressive and how difficult it must be for us to stick to all the rules, but it was selfish of us to act as if the only people who mattered were ourselves and to think that we could do just as we pleased. He told her that he understood that we might think that people like our parents and the mistresses at school were always getting at us, but had she ever asked herself why they were reacting like that? None of us can have exactly what we want all the time, he said, and if you think that's a lot of nonsense, just spare a thought for Wendy. Does she complain or behave badly? All right, so she has a really nice nature and it is more difficult for those of us who are impulsive and find it difficult to control ourselves, but all I ask is that both of you do your best and take time to think about the consequences before you do anything as stupid as that again.'

'How did you take that?'

'I and I believe, Lexie as well, were really upset, mainly, I think, because we knew what her granddad was saying was true and Lexie desperately didn't want to lose his love and help, which she really appreciated.'

'Thank you. What you've just said has been very helpful. One last question; how did you get on with Matthew Travers?'

'I didn't. He just ignored me. Lexie told me not to worry as he was just as bad with her, but in a different way and she hated him.'

'Did she say why?'

'It was a religious thing. He used to call her Jezebel and say that she would go to hell unless she repented and mended her ways. Pompous idiot! Who did he think he was? I can tell you, despite all that holy Joe image of his, he was always sneaking looks at Lexie's cleavage and her bum and tried to pretend that he wasn't.'

Sarah sat for several minutes in the study after Rosie Maxwell had gone and then, her mind made up, went across to the main school building and obtained Sir Michael Travers's phone number from the headmistress's secretary. As luck would have it, he was in, and not only that, suggested that she come over to his house and then have lunch with him.

SIX

SIR MICHAEL WAS a tall, upright man, who looked to be in his late sixties. He had a ready smile and, like his son, was slim, neat and tidy in his brown suit. He was standing at the front door as Sarah drove up and he strode across to the car as it came to a halt and opened the door.

'Obviously you had no trouble in finding the house,' he said with a smile, 'which is a great deal more than can be said of most people. My housekeeper has had to take her daughter, who has Down's Syndrome, to the doctor. Nothing serious, I'm glad to say; just a nasty cold, but it so easily goes to her chest. I thought, therefore, that we should have lunch at the local pub and the bonus will be that we won't be disturbed by the telephone – my life is ruled by the wretched thing. Why don't you drive us straight there and you'll be able to freshen up when we get there?'

The King's Arms was only ten minutes away by car and when they had ordered their lunch at the bar, he showed her to a table in an alcove next to a window with a view of the garden.

'I'm very glad you've come,' he said, after they had tasted their drinks, 'not least because I'd very much welcome a chat about Lexie with someone who's neither connected to the family nor the school. I'm the last person to claim that I'm any sort of expert on the subject of adolescent girls. I do have an unmarried daughter, but, let me put it this way, she always was head prefect material. She is very worthy, but, to be honest, has never been exactly a bundle of fun. I must not mock her, though, she's had a very successful career as a barrister, specializing in company law and is perfectly happy with her life.

'I am only too well aware that there were times when Lexie's behaviour could be intolerable, but I was never on the receiving end of that and she was always lively and full of fun whenever she came here. My son is not one to exaggerate, any more than his mother-in-law, that nice woman Mrs Carlyle, and from what they have said about her, I cannot imagine why they didn't get her seen by an expert in the field of adolescent girls long ago. Unlike them, my daughter-in-law, who sees everything in black and white, seems to believe that Alex was a psychopath and had no moral sense of right and wrong. I don't believe that that was true. You see, she was most patient and really nice to Wendy, the daughter of my resident housekeeper, Mrs Harris, who also lives with us. You see, Wendy, who is just fifteen, has Down's Syndrome and always looked forward to her visits. For her part, Alex was always patient and really nice to her.'

'As you know, Sir Michael, I went to Alex's school earlier today,' Sarah said. 'I saw the headmistress, her housemistress and the girl with whom she was involved in that incident, of which I gather you are well aware. The two women gave me the impression that the incident had been blown up out of all proportion by the student from a teacher training college, Alison Carter, but that was not what Rosie Maxwell had to say to me. Admittedly, I put a bit of pressure on her, but I was left in little doubt that more than just fooling about was involved in that episode in the shower.'

The man smiled. 'I know what happens from time to time at single sex schools – after all I went to one myself. I suspected the same thing and I have no doubt at all that you are right. An environment like that was quite wrong for Alex and the combination of someone like her, who had a strong personality and an even stronger libido, with someone pliant and impressionable like her friend, Rosie Maxwell, was always playing with fire. Rosie came to stay here with Alex a couple of times and I could see the potential for trouble straight away, sensing that their relationship was a bit more than mere friendship, and so I took certain precautions. The wing in which Mrs Harris and Wendy live can be isolated by just one door, which Mrs Harris likes to keep locked as Wendy had been known to wander at night. It has a spare bedroom in it and she was only too happy for Rosie to sleep in her part of the house. I have no idea whether either of the girls suspected what I was up to, but on both weekends the two of them were on their best behaviour.

'As far as the incident at the school was concerned, I tackled both of them together, pointing out how close to disaster they had been and that there was to be no repeat of it. I like to believe that they took it all in and I had promises that nothing like that would happen again at the school.

'They both came to stay with me for one last weekend after that and Lexie was very sensible, or some would say rather clever, with me and freely admitted what they had been doing, that she was very sorry and that there would be no repeat of it. Rosie went a lot further and said that she had decided to keep her distance from Lexie during term time and not to see her at all during the holidays after that visit to me.

'Would it have worked? I like to think so and certainly there was no further trouble with the two of them at the school for the rest of that term.'

'Did you have any ideas why Alex behaved the way she did?'

'Believe me, I have given a great deal of thought to that. I am a lay member of the academic board of one of the hospitals in Oxford and I went as far as to have a chat to one of the psychiatrists there, who specializes in adolescents, saying that I was concerned about the general and in particular, the sexual behaviour of one of the girls at the school of which I was chairman of the board. Up to a point, you will know by now that that is the truth, but I was not prepared to risk even hinting that it was my grand-daughter, Alex.'

'What did he say?'

'As I had told him that the girl had been adopted and that nothing was known about her parentage, he said that hereditary factors might have been playing a part; other possibilities were that she was suffering from a bipolar disorder, which, as I'm sure you know, used to be known as manic depression. Lastly, he said that it would be worth trying to find out if she had suffered any form of birth injury to the brain, as from what I had said it appeared that she had been the same from a very young age. Finally, he strongly recommended that, in the first place, she be referred to a neurologist and if that and any investigations were negative, a psychiatrist, preferably a woman with particular experience of adolescent girls. Although what he said made excellent sense, I knew only too well that both my son and daughter-in-law would find it very difficult to swallow that and as Lexie seemed to have settled down a bit after that incident at school, I put the idea on hold.'

'Obviously,' Sarah said, 'everyone in your son's house is still in a state of shock. How do you think they will take this tragedy in the long run?'

'I believe that the short answer to that is pretty much as they have done already. My son is by no means an unfeeling person, but neither is he emotional and however upset he may be about what happened to Alex, that must be tinged with some relief. She was undoubtedly a potential loose cannon as far as his career was concerned; he coped very well with both what happened in Corfu and at the school, but he must have worried that his future in politics might be compromised if she carried on like that and the press got to hear about it, which, I have to say, seemed more than likely.

'Madeleine is not the most patient of women and I believe that she had rather given up on Alex, leaving her management largely to Richard and that nice woman, her mother. She very much sees everything in black and white and seemed to me to have taken the view that Alex was impossible, that she had tried her hardest to cope with her and as her mother clearly thought she could do better, then the best thing would be to leave the care of the girl to her. I don't hold with many of Madeleine's views and certainly not the mess she made of managing Alex and to some extent Matthew as well. It is clear to me that her taking a strict religious line with an impressionable adolescent like Alex was little short of a disaster.

'It was Mrs Carlyle who, in my opinion, was the one person in that household who provided the love and guidance that Alex so desperately needed. She also had the ability to calm her down and, if necessary, reason with her effectively. She is already supplying the same love and support to Lizzie and that will help her, too, although having said that, she is a fundamentally happy child, perhaps too young to have taken it all in and I have no real worries about her.

'Apart from that business at Alex's school, I have always felt it best not to stick my oar into matters associated with my son's marriage. Anyway, Maddy will certainly not fall apart as the result of what happened to Alex, nor, do I believe, will Mrs Carlyle, although she is bound to be extremely upset as she really loved the girl, which I know was reciprocated.

'The person in that household about whom I am most concerned is Matthew. He clearly resented Alex's arrival, hardly surprising as, at the time, he was a shy 7-year-old who, even at that age, disliked displays of emotion. She was two years younger than him and was virtually out of control, overly affectionate on occasions, and flying into rages or having bouts of desperate misery, at others. He reacted by having as little to do with her as possible. He managed to persuade his parents to send him to a boarding preparatory school and during the holidays, he either shut himself in his room, reading or playing chess against the CD on his computer or going to suitable holiday camps for boys. He became obsessed with religion, like his mother, who no doubt influenced him in his feelings towards Alex, clearly seeing her as being possessed by the Devil. He is a clever boy, nice looking and good at games, but, dare I say it, he is joyless. I don't think that sending him to the same school that both Richard and I attended was a good idea, either. It suited Richard down to the ground. Personable, never taking life too seriously, but with a social conscience, good at games and with a very clear idea of what he was going to do, he sailed through his time there. He also has a well developed sense of humour, an attribute which unfortunately Matthew lacks completely. The boy is already talking about taking holy orders himself. In my view, it is far too early for him to be thinking on those lines and instead he should be getting experience of life.

'Had Matthew been my son, I would long since have taken him away from the college and I even spoke to Richard about my anxieties. However, he takes a much more relaxed attitude about him than me and believes that it is just a phase and as the young man gets older he will take a more balanced view of things. I very much hope that he's right, but somehow I doubt it.'

'Have you spoken to Matthew since the tragedy?'

'Only on the telephone and I'm afraid I wasn't able to help him all that much. I said that it was quite natural for him to be terribly upset about Alex, we all were, and that the fact that he disapproved of her in many ways, made it all that more difficult to cope with. He hardly said anything in response, but I knew that he was due to go back to school shortly after it had happened and under the circumstances getting away from home seemed to me, on balance, the best thing for him to do.'

'My colleague, Inspector Sinclair, is going up to the school today and plans to see both him and his housemaster,' Sarah said.

'I've met Gerald Fisher a few times. He is an excellent man, distinctly less rigid in his views than many of the other masters there and Matthew will be in good hands. As for Richard, he asked for my view about whether it would be better for him to go back to school for the time being and be kept occupied or stay at home. I was strongly in favour of the former and I'm glad to say that that was Richard's view, too.'

'How did Matthew take that decision?'

'All I know is what Richard told me on the phone and that was that Matthew seemed relieved to be getting away from the house where the terrible event had taken place.'

Sarah was on her way back to Mrs Sinclair's house, when she saw the signpost to the Traverses village. Glancing at the clock on the dashboard and seeing that it was just past 4.15, she decided that this might be as good a time as any to have a chat with Lizzie, who should be back at the house from her primary school.

Mrs Carlyle, who was reading a book on the terrace at the back of the house, smiled and waved as Sarah came round the side of the house on the path from the drive at the front.

'Would you like a cup of tea?' she asked.

'That's very kind of you, but I had a very late lunch and a coffee after it. I just want to have a brief chat with Lizzie. I won't raise anything contentious, but we can't afford to ignore any clue, however slight and she might just have noticed something unusual the morning that dreadful thing happened.'

'I hate to have to ask you this, but does Madeleine know that you might be talking to her?'

'I imagine so, because we mentioned the possibility quite specifically to Mr Travers. He had no objection and no doubt he passed that on to your daughter.'

The woman smiled. 'That's all right, then. I felt I had to ask as I have to tread a little carefully with Madeleine at times; she gets a bit touchy if she thinks I'm taking over. Why not see Lizzie now? She's on the swing over there.' Anne Carlyle glanced at her watch. 'I've promised to help her with her sewing before supper and if you are through by 5.15, that will give us enough time. I'll read my book here until you've finished.'

The small girl gave Sarah a smile as she approached and allowed the swing to slow down.

'Hello. My name is Sarah and I work for the police. I've already seen your dad in his office in the village and he's quite happy for us to chat to you about Lexie.' Sarah turned and looked round for a moment. 'Why don't we sit on that bench over there? Your gran will be able to see us and let us know when it's time for you to do your sewing.'

The small girl happily took Sarah's hand and skipped along beside her as they made their way to the garden seat.

'Did you see Lexie on the morning she was hurt?' Sarah asked.

'Just at breakfast. She had promised to help me with my tennis practice afterwards, but after I had done my teeth, I couldn't find her down by the court and I decided to have a swing instead. You see, we had a silly argument at breakfast; Mum lost her temper, spilt the milk over the table and sent Lexie up to her room. I didn't see her after that and wondered if Mum had given her a spanking in there, or something. She did that to her sometimes when she got very cross with her.'

'Who told you that?'

'Lexie. I knew that it used to happen to children a long time ago 'cos my gran reads me stories from the books about schools that she has kept ever since she was a little girl and there were spankings in them. She told me that it was no longer allowed. I was telling Lexie about the book and she said that that wasn't true as Mum had just done it to her. I didn't believe her and told her so.'

'What did she do then?'

'She said that she could prove it and I bet her that she couldn't. "How much?" she said. We agreed on a bar of chocolate that I had been keeping and she lifted up her skirt, pulled down her pants and turned round. It looked really bad and when I asked her if she had cried, she said: "I never cry when she does that".'

'Did your gran know about it?'

'I don't know.'

'Did you see anyone while you were out here the morning that Lexie died?'

'Just the gardeners and Matthew. He came out on to the terrace, walked across to the swing and got me going really high. After that, I thought I'd show him the fuchsia I've been growing for my gran. It's her seventieth birthday soon. I'm going to buy a pot to put it in and my mum has promised to take me to the garden centre to find a really nice one in good time. I've been saving up for it for ages and I know she'll love it. She knows a lot about flowers and Phil told me that fuchsias were her favourites.'

'You like Phil, do you?'

'Oh, yes. He's ever so nice and Gran likes him, too.'

'How about Mr Palmer?'

'He's a bit grumpy, but Gran thinks he's a really good gardener. She told me that his bark was worse than his bite.' The small girl giggled. 'I thought that was really funny thing to say and I put it into a story we were told to write at school. Miss Sturrock, our English teacher, mentioned it specially to the class and gave us lots of other things like that to write down. The one I liked best was "a storm in a teacup". I thought of that when Mum got so cross with us at breakfast that morning and spilt the milk.'

'How do you get on with Matthew?'

'He's all right, but he always looks so miserable and he never smiles much, unlike Dad and my gran and granddad. I told my mum once that Gran and Granddad ought to get married and she got really cross, telling me not to be so silly. I thought it was a really good idea.'

'How about Lexie and Matthew?'

'He never said anything about her to me, but Lexie hated him.'

'Did she say why?'

'Just that he was always so miserable, never smiled and was always telling her how silly and childish she was.'

'Did he ever have friends to stay here?'

'No, but Lexie did, a friend from her school. I didn't like her.'

'Why not?'

'She was snooty and wouldn't talk to me.'

'I'm quite sure that you two will be wanting to discuss what you've been doing today,' Mrs Sinclair said after they had finished their dinner that evening. 'Why not go out on to the terrace while I do the washing up and I'll bring you a pot of coffee and a slab of that dark chocolate you're so fond of, Mark?'

'We wouldn't dream of it, Ma, would we, Sarah?'

'Certainly not. The three of us would make short work of it, but so would two and you've done everything up to now.'

Mrs Sinclair smiled at them. 'Let's call a truce. You two can do the washing up and I'll put everything away and get the coffee.'

'Done,' Mark said, giving her a hug.

Half an hour later, they were sitting on a bench on the terrace, which had an uninterrupted view of the back garden and the trees beyond.

'Why don't I go first?' Sinclair said. 'I didn't spend all that much time at the College, but it was interesting nonetheless.

He described his meeting with Matthew's housemaster, Gerald Fisher, on his own and then the further one with the boy and Hughes, the chaplain.

'I'm very concerned about young Matthew. He seems to be completely in thrall to that chaplain, who started to behave like a nit-picking solicitor, attempting to prevent his client from giving anything away, that is until I got all official with him. I wasn't the only one, either; Fisher is obviously equally worried about the boy. I thought it sense not to push too hard, but it strikes me that it would be very much in Matthew's interest to get away from the college for a bit and I would be very interested to hear from you what you made of Sir Michael, as his place seems as good a one for the young man to go to as any. Matthew was extremely edgy when I talked to him and if we can get him away from that chaplain, I have an instinct that he might have something more to tell us.'

'I was very impressed by Sir Michael,' Sarah said. 'Not only did I like him personally, but he obviously had an excellent relationship with Lexie and from what her friend Rosie said, she behaved much more sensibly with him than with her immediate family.'

'I'm very glad to hear that. If we are going to interview Matthew properly, we need to get both his father and grandfather on our side. Perhaps we should put the idea to Richard Travers as soon as possible.'

'Yes, I think we should. Do you feel strong enough to do the talking? I got a distinct feeling the last time we saw him that he relates better to men than women, at least when talking about his family.'

'All right, but I don't exactly relish it.'

'So you've made some progress, have you?' Richard Travers said when they met him at his office at 8.30 the following morning, half an hour before he was due to start his surgery with his constituents.

'Yes, sir, we have. Following inspection of that boulder above the pond and the results of the autopsy, we have concluded that Alex was sunbathing in the nude and reading her book and then probably heard something behind her. She appears to have got to her feet and was then knocked unconscious by a blow to her face when standing facing her assailant, from some form of blunt instrument, possibly a fist, although the forensic pathologist wasn't sure. She fell sideways, face down into the water and drowned as a result.'

'Had she been interfered with sexually?'

'No, there was nothing to suggest that, but as you are already aware, there is no doubt that she had been active in that way previously.'

'And your other inquiries?'

'We had discussions with your wife, your mother-in-law and father as well as having visited both Alex's and Matthew's schools. My colleague had very useful talks with Alex's headmistress, her housemistress, Miss Lake and her friend, Rosie Maxwell, and finally with your father, who was clearly instrumental in dealing with that shower episode, about which I am sure you are familiar. As for me, I was extremely concerned about Matthew when I saw him in the presence of his housemaster and the assistant chaplain, one Ian Hughes.'

'In what way?'

'He behaved more like Matthew's solicitor than his religious mentor. Evidently your son has been in a very disturbed state of mind ever since returning to school; he has been going to see Hughes frequently and seems extremely anxious. I didn't think it wise to try to find out exactly why he was so upset. Of course, I fully understand that the tragedy of Alex's death must have hit him hard, particularly, perhaps, as it seems obvious that the two of them didn't get on, but I felt that there was more to it than that. Whatever the reason, I am concerned about his mental state. However, he was in the house at the time of Alex's death and we do need to hear his account of her state of mind at breakfast that morning when I gather she was behaving badly and he appears to have been feeling unwell.'

'We were also wondering about the possibility of Matthew spending some time with his grandfather. Perhaps we might have a talk to him there with both you and your father present.'

'I, too, am worried about Matthew and indeed Gerald Fisher rang me up after your visit, to tell me that his return to school had not gone well. I would like to get my father's view of all this and to that end, propose to telephone him right now. Perhaps you wouldn't mind going into the waiting room while I do so.'

'Of course not,' Sinclair replied.

A good fifteen minutes went by before Travers returned. 'In principle both my father and I agree that some time away from the college would be in Matthew's interest and that the arrangements should be made as soon possible. After some discussion, we also felt that it would be best for him go to my father's house, as you suggested. He would be free from the constant reminder of what happened at my place and it would be much quieter. From my point of view, too, it would be the best solution. At my house there would be the constant threat of press interest and I don't think it would be fair to put any further load on to my mother-in-law. Madeleine has a number of engagements that she would prefer not to cancel – and I am also well aware that Matthew's moodiness and now his obvious depression would get her down, and that in itself would certainly not help him either. Apart from that, my mother-in-law has quite enough on her hands looking after Lizzie and getting on with Madeleine, without Matthew as well. I am quite sure, too, that you must be aware that there has been friction between the two of them for some time now. That has largely been due to disagreement over the best way to handle Alex and I believe that it will take some time to sort things out.'

'You may be wondering why I can't take some leave now to sort all this out, but that is quite impossible. I am due to accompany the prime minister to a meeting with the French and German presidents early next week and with all the background work I have done on the particular problem, I can't possibly duck out of it at this stage.

'If you would let me have your mobile number, I'll ring you as soon as I have definite news for you and when a time for an interview with Matthew is possible for everyone concerned.'

'That's very good of you, sir, we look forward to hearing from you.'

*

'I think I'll have a go at my mother's lawn while I'm waiting to hear from Travers,' Sinclair said. 'She does have a man who comes once a month to see to it, but he's not due for a couple of weeks and it's looking distinctly shaggy. How about you?'

'I'll take the opportunity to have a word with the domestic staff at the house on their own – it's about time I did so.'

Sarah decided to telephone the house, being prepared to ring off should anyone other than the housekeeper or the cook answer. As she had hoped, it was the former.

'Mrs Weston, this is Inspector Prescott speaking.'

'Yes, madam, how may I help you?'

'I wonder if I might have a quiet chat with you as soon as possible at a time when you are on your own and we won't be disturbed.'

There was a short pause. 'Mrs Travers has gone to a meeting in Oxford today and I'm not expecting her back until the late afternoon and Mrs Carlyle will be at Lizzie's sports day this afternoon at her school. Apart from the gardening staff, I will be alone here from two o'clock onwards as it is Mrs Parsmore's afternoon off.'

'That would suit me very well and I'll be with you soon after two. I'll let you have my mobile number in case there is any change in anyone's plans.'

'Very good, madam.'

*

Sarah decided to park her car well away from the house. She rang the front doorbell soon after the time the house-keeper had mentioned and was shown into the woman's small sitting room off the kitchen.

'It's very good of you to see me. I'm anxious to get as accurate an account of what happened on the morning of Alex's tragic death as I can and I wonder if you'd take me through anything out of the ordinary that happened that morning. I understand that Mr Travers left quite early.'

'Yes, that's right, madam. I brought his usual morning meal of fresh grapefruit, cereal, toast and coffee to the breakfast room at seven and he went off in his car at about half past. He leaves it in the station car park if he is just going up to London for the day.'

'Did he seem his usual self?'

'Oh, yes. He's a very even-tempered and pleasant man is Mr Travers. He always has a smile and a few words to say to me before he leaves on those days when he has breakfast on his own. That day he was his usual self and I remember his asking if I had been disturbed by the thunderstorm during the night.'

'I understand that there was something of a row at the breakfast table when the others came down later.'

'Yes, that often seemed to happen when Mr Travers wasn't there. You see, Lexie and Lizzie used to wind each other up and, although I probably shouldn't say this, Mrs Travers isn't at her best early in the morning and she wasn't very good at dealing with them, particularly as far as Lexie was concerned. That morning was typical. About twenty minutes after I had left the breakfast room having taken in the coffee pot for Mrs Travers, Matthew came into the kitchen to ask me for a dish cloth, telling me that his mother had spilt the milk all over the table and broken the glass jug. He didn't exactly spell out the details, just saying that she had lost her temper with Alex and Lizzie, who had been quarrelling.'

'Did he say what they were quarrelling about?'

'Oh, just who should have the fruit salad that Matthew couldn't face as he had woken with a bit of a stomach upset. Evidently their mother was shouting at them, leaned across the table to take hold of the bowl herself and that's when she knocked over the milk jug and it broke. That's when she sent Matthew out to the kitchen to get a cloth to mop it up.'

'Did Matthew look unwell?'

'He certainly did. He was as white as a sheet and told me that he was feeling sick, so I suggested that he went up to his room to lie down and that I'd come up to see how he was after I'd dealt with the mess in the breakfast room.'

'And did you?'

'Yes, but he wasn't there and I assumed that he had gone out for a breath of fresh air instead. Anyway, before that, on my way to the breakfast room, I passed Mrs Travers in the hall and she was clearly beside herself with rage. She completely ignored me and went into the drawing room, slamming the door behind her.'

'What time was that?'

'It must have been between half past eight and quarter to nine. Anyway, when I went into the breakfast room, Lizzie was in there alone, crying, and there was milk all over the tablecloth with the jug in three pieces. It could have been a lot worse; none of the milk had gone on to the carpet, there were no splinters of glass and it wasn't as if the table was anything special. I managed to calm Lizzie down by getting her to help me and then took her up to Mrs Carlyle's flat. What made it easier was that it had already been arranged that she should look after Lizzie while Mrs Travers went off to some meeting in Oxford.'

'Did you tell Mrs Carlyle what had happened?'

'No, Lizzie had settled down and I didn't want to set her off again. Anyway, I had just started across the landing towards Matthew's room to see if he was all right, but there was no answer to my knock and at the same time Alex passed me on her way down from the floor above. She was wearing a wrap, a sun hat and canvas shoes and by the look of her not much else and was carrying a book and a towel.

'"I'm just off for a sunbathe, Mrs W," she said giving me one of her radiant smiles. She didn't look as if she had a care in the world.

'I remember offering up a silent prayer that her mother wouldn't see where she was going, as at times Mrs Travers has a violent temper and was quite capable of beating Alex and, indeed, I had heard her doing so only a few months back. I have to say that it didn't seem to have worried Alex all that much, because when her mother had gone I went in to see if the girl was all right and she wasn't crying or anything. I asked her what she had done to deserve a beating like that, but she said she couldn't tell me, although I had already guessed, having heard her at it on a number of other occasions. I'm sorry to be so coy about it, but my generation's like that.'

'That's all right, I know just what you mean. Did you notice what time it was that you saw Alex coming down the stairs?'

'It must have been a minute or two after nine o'clock, because when Mrs Carlyle opened the door to my knock, the news headlines were being read on Classic FM, which she always liked to have on over her breakfast.'

'So she gets that herself, does she?'

'Yes. She just likes to have cereal, fruit juice, an apple and toast with her coffee, while she listens to the music on the radio.'

'How do you get on with Mrs Travers?'

'She treats me like a servant in one of those costume dramas on TV, ordering me about without so much as a please or a thank you. If it hadn't been for the rest of the family, particularly Mrs Carlyle, I probably would have left long ago. She's a really lovely lady and I often have chats with her and she lets me have the magazines she takes after she has finished with them. She also knew exactly how to cope with Alex and had the knack of calming her down when she was having one of her emotional crises. I also like Mr Travers, who always has a kind word and a smile for me and gives me a really lovely present every Christmas. Lizzie is a nice little girl, too, and although Alex could be moody and sad at times, mostly she was really good fun and I hated the way her mother treated her.'

'How about Matthew?'

'I've never been able to make him out at all. He never seems to smile, have fun or really enjoy anything. Mrs Travers was very strict with him when he was younger and used to beat him, too, and perhaps that had something to do with it. I know that I ought to have spoken to Mr Travers about it, because I hate the very idea of that happening to any child, but I couldn't afford to lose this job, which I most certainly would have done if his wife got to hear that I had done so. It is not only well paid, but is close to the old peoples' home where my old mother is and I knew that my chances of finding anything nearly as convenient in the vicinity would be small. I did, though, tell Mrs Carlyle about the time her daughter beat Alex and afterwards she really let her have it. I didn't hear exactly what she said – Mrs Travers was shouting back at her to start with, but that soon stopped and when she left the room a few minutes later, she looked really shaken. Mrs

Carlyle is like that. She never raises her voice, but in her quiet way has real authority.'

'Has anyone told you any details about what happened to Alex down by the pool?'

'I heard a bit about it from Mrs Carlyle when she asked me to run a bath for Phil Rouse when he came up to the house soaking wet, but nothing much more than that he had found Lexie under the water in the pool, that he had pulled her out, but she was already dead.'

'Thank you, Mrs Weston, you've been very helpful. I'm sure you won't take it amiss if I ask you not to say anything about what we have been discussing, not even to Mrs Carlyle. I want you to be particularly on your guard with any strangers who might call, too, either on the phone or in person. One never knows with the press; they can not only be very persuasive, but can also catch one unawares if one is not on one's guard. They can also be very plausible and I've come across them pretending to be anything from friends of the family to salesmen.'

'I'll be very careful.'

'Good. I'm sure you will.'

SEVEN

MATTHEW TRAVERS, SINCLAIR thought, looked absolutely terrible when he came into Sir Michael Travers's drawing room the evening of the following day, accompanied by his father, to join his grandfather and the two detectives. He was as pale as a ghost and a tiny muscle was twitching under his left eye.

'We are well aware,' Sinclair said, after he had introduced Sarah to him, 'that you have been extremely upset by what happened to Alex and we have no intention of adding to your distress unnecessarily, but I hope you understand that we are in the process of talking to all the members of your father's household, including all the domestic and gardening staff, and naturally we have to include you. I judged that you were not in a fit state to tell me all about it when I saw you at your school, but I gather that you are feeling less distressed now and are slowly coming to terms with what happened. We are anxious to discover exactly what occurred the morning that Alex died and at the same time to help you to get over it, as you are so obviously and understandably upset. We understand that she was playing up a bit at breakfast that morning. Perhaps, as a start you would tell us about that.'

Sinclair saw the young man glance in his father's direction, who gave an almost imperceptible nod, and then he began.

Things got off to a bad start for Matthew Travers on that terrible morning when everything else seemed to go wrong, too. He had woken with a stomach ache and was still feeling queasy when he went down to breakfast at eight. His father was not there, having caught the early train for London, and that in itself was not a good sign. When he was present, almost always quietly reading the morning paper, Alex and Lizzie were on their best behaviour, but when he was not, the two of them almost invariably quarrelled or provoked one another. That morning was no exception. They were having a stupid argument about who should have his portion of fruit salad, which he couldn't face, and there was something of a tug-of-war going on with his bowl between the two of them.

'Stop it, you two!' their mother shouted, her cheeks flushed with anger.

She had been in a foul mood ever since she had come into the room and she hit the table with her fist so hard that all the crockery rattled. Seeing that the milk jug was in danger of falling over, she made a grab for it, but misjudged the distance, knocking it over. It hit the teapot hard and broke into three pieces and the contents ran over the tablecloth.

'Now look what you've made me do. It was all your fault, Alexandra, and I've had enough of your bad behaviour. Go up to your room at once and you know what to expect when I deal with you later.'

Alex flounced out of the room and as she slammed the door after her, his mother turned towards him and said:

'Don't sit there staring at me like that, Matthew! Go and fetch a cloth from the kitchen.'

He was only too glad to leave the room, as at any moment he thought he was going to be sick.

'Don't you worry, Mr Matthew,' the housekeeper said, when he had told her what had happened. 'You're as white as a sheet – I'll deal with it. Why don't you go up to your room and lie down for a bit?'

After she had left the room and reached the hall, he started towards the staircase, but didn't think he was going to make it up there in time as the waves of nausea spread through him, so instead he hurried to the cloak-room near the door that led out on to the terrace and the back garden. For a few moments he sat on the lavatory seat, feeling the sweat on his forehead and after what seemed like an age, although it could only have been about ten minutes, he began to feel a bit better and he got up, opened the window a crack and bathed his face in cold water in the basin. He had just started to dry himself with the towel, when he heard the door to the terrace being opened, and pulling back the curtain and looking out, he saw Lexie walking across the terrace, carrying a towel and a book and then running down the steps on to the lawn. She was wearing a thin robe and a sun hat and he could hear her whistling and looking as if she hadn't a care in the world as she walked across the grass towards the pond.

Soon after, still not feeling himself, he remained sitting on the lavatory seat and some fifteen minutes later was just thinking about going up to his bedroom, when he heard someone come into the outer cloakroom, where there were pegs set into a strip of wood fastened to the wall, on which hung rainwear. There was also a large cylindrical container on the floor in which was a variety of walking sticks and umbrellas.

It could only have been his mother and when he was quite sure that she had left and wasn't coming back, he went out there himself. He hadn't noticed it before on his way to the lavatory, but now he saw the crook-handled cane in the container. How he hated the wretched thing, remembering only too well how his mother had used it on him when he was younger. Had she taken it out earlier and then beaten Lexie with it as a punishment for her behaviour in the breakfast room? Was that what she meant when she said that she would deal with her later?

It seemed only too likely, and after he had waited for a

good further twenty minutes, sitting on the lavatory seat and being satisfied that she wasn't coming back, as well as feeling quite a bit better, he went out on to the terrace to get some fresh air. Seeing Lizzie on the swing, he suddenly decided to go over and give her a push. Ever since the holiday in Corfu, when he had been spending a lot of time with her on the beach, he had been getting on better with her and perhaps that would help him to get his mind off it all. It worked; Lizzie was her usual cheerful self and after a few minutes, he felt much better and agreed to her suggestion that he should have a look at the fuchsia she had been growing for her grandma's birthday.

Feeling less nauseous and calmer in himself, he told his little sister how lovely her plant was and then made his way up to his room and tried to take his mind off what had happened by doing some revision. He wasn't sure how long he had been doing that before he heard the pounding on the door to the terrace, followed by the sound of voices from downstairs. From the landing, he saw his grandmother by the telephone in the hall and when she rang off, he called down to ask her what was wrong.

'Lexie's had an accident by the pool,' she said, 'and I've sent for an ambulance. Don't worry, there's nothing you can do. It's best if we don't get in the way and wait until it comes.'

He only heard of the full horror of what had happened, when, a long time later, his grandmother came up to his room and although she didn't give him any details, she told him that Lexie was dead. He couldn't take it in and the nightmare continued. No one would tell him in detail what had happened and he kept out of the way as much as possible until two days later, when the detective found him trying to practise his golf at the net. At least, the man was relaxed and pleasant to him and gave him some hints about his swing. His worry increased, though, with the arrival of the same detective at his school. Surely, he thought, they didn't suspect that he had had anything to do with Lexie's death. He felt terrible about the fact that not only had he disliked her, but he had grown to hate her. He wasn't made of stone and the way she flaunted her body in front of him distressed him greatly, particularly the realization of just how much it excited him.

At first, his return to school had been a relief, as Mr Hughes, the assistant chaplain, whom he went to see and was the only person in whom he felt able to confide, was a comfort to him. But then the man wouldn't leave him alone, constantly questioning him about the way his mother had treated him, wanting to know exactly what she had done after the times she beat him, making insinuations that weren't true both about her and also about what he himself had done or wanted to do to Lexie. It was almost as if the priest was enjoying hearing about it and it even seemed as if the man was trying to put words into his mouth. Was he going mad? Surely a chaplain wouldn't behave like that and had he imagined or misinterpreted some of the things the man questioned him about?

The detective's visit to the school added to his anxiety and worry, but the talk his housemaster had had with him the following day was a great relief. The man told him that he had come back to school too soon after the tragic events at his home and how would he view going to stay with his grandfather, for whom he personally had the highest regard, for a time, in order to relax and come to terms with the tragedy that had occurred? Matthew asked Mr Fisher if he could think the suggestion over, but he didn't really need to, knowing straight away that it would be the best thing for him. He was very fond of his grandfather, who was such a warm and friendly man, and if anyone could help him, it would be he. He went the very next day.

His grandfather didn't say a great deal himself, merely telling him that as he was so upset, it would be best if he rested quietly for a day or two. Inevitably, he explained, the police would want to talk to him about what had happened to Alex, as they had to everyone else in the family, but the detective had agreed that both he and his father would be allowed to be present when that happened. He must of course tell them the absolute truth.

Matthew had been dreading that his grandfather might insist that his mother should be there as well, but when he was told that that would not be the case, he was unable to hide his sigh of relief, knowing that he would never have

been able to face her. Desperately nervous at first, he gradually began to relax as he repeated what had happened.

'I swear that I have told you the absolute truth,' the boy
said after he had finished, looking directly at the two detectives, a tear slowly coursing its way down his right cheek.
'You do believe me, don't you?'

'The two of us with your father and grandfather, will need
to consider the implications of what you have told us very
carefully, as I'm sure you understand,' Sinclair said. 'But I
for one, think it very brave of you to have been so frank with
us. It's just possible that we will need to ask you some more
questions later, but I hope that that won't be necessary. In
the meantime, we believe that it would make sense for you
to stay here with your grandfather for a few more days,
provided, of course, that he agrees.'

Sir Michael smiled at his grandson. 'Of course, I'd be
delighted for you to stay as long as you like, Matthew, and
it'll give us a chance to see what can be done about that golf
swing of yours. Now, why not go up to bed? I'm sure you
could do with a decent night's sleep.'

'Good idea,' Travers said, getting to his feet and putting
his arm round his son's shoulders, 'I'll take you up there.'

The man returned within a few minutes. 'I think he'll be
all right now that he's got all that stuff off his chest. The big
question now is where does Madeleine stand in all this?'

Sinclair nodded. 'One thing that concerns me particularly

about what Matthew told us just now is that your wife, Mr Travers, could not possibly have been in any way involved with Alex's death. You see, she told me that she had stopped for petrol at your local garage, where she is very well known, on her way to Oxford for her meeting the morning of Alex's death. She paid with her debit card, but mislaid the receipt. However, when I checked with the proprietor, he located his copy, which showed that she had operated the machine that morning at 8.58. Now, Alex was seen by the housekeeper going down the stairs in her wrap on her way to sunbathe at almost exactly nine o'clock that morning. She passed Mrs Weston very close to Mrs Carlyle's half open door and the woman quite clearly heard the announcer on Classic FM reading the news headlines.

'Why, then, did Matthew suggest that she had been in the cloakroom some time well after nine o'clock and what about that cane that he claims had been used by her to beat him in the past? I have to say, though, that both Mrs Carlyle and Mrs Weston told us that your wife had used corporal punishment on both him and Alex in the past.'

There was a long pause, then Richard Travers said: 'What you have just told us disturbs me more than I can say and I had no idea that Madeleine had done that. I am also well aware that that method of punishment is illegal now and in any case would have been quite unacceptable to me even if that had not been the case.'

'But you did know that the cane was there?'

'Yes, but I had completely forgotten about it. Let me explain. You see, in my father's time at the College, beating was still carried out a lot as a form of discipline and the boy who was head of the house, was allowed to do so as well as the housemaster. It was when my father was in that position himself that corporal punishment was abandoned for boys on boys and then altogether some years after that. He took his house cane home as a souvenir and then gave it to me as a bit of past history as I had told him that I was thinking of writing a memoir about my own time at the college. I never got round to doing that and until just now I'd forgotten about that cane altogether. I suppose that from time to time I must have noticed its presence in the cloak-room, but it became part of the furniture, so to speak, and it never occurred to me that Madeleine might have used it on Matthew, let alone Alex. Indeed, I had forgotten about it altogether until just now when Matthew was telling us about it.'

'And you no doubt remember giving it to your son, Sir Michael?' Sinclair said.

'I certainly do and I'm horrified to hear what you have discovered about its use,' the man replied. 'I only brought it back from the College as a souvenir and a reminder of how barbarous discipline was in those days. My son and I will see that it is broken up and burnt as soon as possible.'

'I'm afraid that we will have to take charge of it until such time as our inquiries are complete and to that end I suggest we follow you back to his house and do so this evening.'

'Yes, I understand that you will need to do that,' Sir Michael said, 'but I'm sure I have no need to point out that any publicity over this would do both my son and me serious damage.'

'Yes, of course, I am fully aware of that and will bear it in mind.'

'Have you any other leads you are following up over this tragic affair?'

'Yes, but for the moment my colleague and I are unable to discuss them with you. I assure you that we will do so as soon as possible.'

'And Richard and I will have to have a long think about how to handle Matthew. What you have told us disturbs me deeply and the only way I can see to resolve it is for the two of us to confront him with the lies he told us and come back to you in the light of what we discover. You don't think he killed Alex, do you?'

'Believe me,' Sinclair said, 'I fully understand the distress that all this is causing you, but we still have further inquiries to pursue. I'll let you know at once of any further developments, although at this stage I can't give you any guarantee when that will be.'

'Although Matthew didn't go as far as to say that he had seen his mother in the cloakroom after Alex had gone down to the pond, he most certainly implied it,' Sarah said when they were on their way back to Mrs Sinclair's house in the car.

'Yes and I'm quite sure that he was lying and I suspect that he saw it as a way of getting his own back on her and letting his father and grandfather know that she had beaten both him and Lexie in the past. He may, of course, have been making up a lot of the other stuff and he is, in my view, still very very much in the frame.'

'What next?'

'Why don't we sleep on it and as tomorrow's Sunday, it'll give us a chance to decide what to do next.'

The two detectives managed to put the case right out of their minds until the following evening. They had woken to find the weather warm and sunny and at breakfast on the terrace overlooking the lawn at the back of his mother's house, Sinclair looked across at his partner.

'I don't suppose you have forgotten the "full docking manoeuvres" we carried out together in Cambridge when we were working on the Professor Vaughan case? I recall a certain interlude under a convenient willow after the exertions of punting up the river towards Grantchester.'

Sarah choked on her coffee and after Mark had thumped her on the back and she had wiped her streaming eyes with her napkin, she shook her head.

'Where on earth did you come across that disgusting expression, you horrible man?'

'In Montacute House, a National Trust property in Somerset. You see, one Eleanor Glyn, who was the mistress of Lord Curzon when he was living at the house, wrote spicy books and some of them are preserved there as well as one of the reviews, which I read with considerable interest, as you may imagine. That particular phrase was obviously used as a euphemism for the shenanigans that the heroine was getting up to in various situations, the most notorious of which was on a tiger skin and resulted in the jingle that went the rounds at the time:

'Would you like to sin with Eleanor Glyn on a tiger skin,
or would you prefer to sin with her, on some other fur.'

'Anyway, I just thought the idea might tickle your fancy, if not in a punt, perhaps in a more appropriate location.'

Sarah just managed not to collapse into another fit of the giggles. 'I'm all for it.'

'Why don't we take a picnic and see if we can hire a punt on the Cherwell. It might bring back memories and whet your appetite for some more strenuous exercise later on in a more discreet location and perhaps not in a punt? We got away with it once, but the stakes now are higher than they were then and just think what a meal our friend Watson would make out of it if he got to hear about it.'

'It doesn't bear thinking about it. Perhaps your mother even has a tiger skin hidden up in her attic. She was in

India with your father for a time after the war, wasn't she?'

'Good idea! Why don't I ask her now and she might give it a spring clean, for us.'

Sarah slapped him hard on the top of his thigh. 'Don't you dare!'

Mrs Sinclair provided them with a picnic and a bottle of hock and all their tensions melted away during that magical afternoon and what followed when they got back.

'I'm still concerned about Palmer and that garden centre,' Sinclair said at breakfast on the Monday, the following morning. 'With Alex's death having been fixed at 9.41, he seems to have had a cast iron alibi as far as her murder is concerned, as he was having a cosy chat with the cook, Mrs Parsmore, at the time, but was he spying on the girl, when she was cavorting with Rosie Maxwell near the pool back in August? Even if he was, what has that to do with her later murder? Be that as it may, I can't think of anything else useful for us to do at present, so why don't we check it out.'

'Good idea.'

They found the garden centre without difficulty and met the director, who introduced them to George Foster, the salesman who dealt with lawn mowers.

'Yes,' he said, 'I do remember Mr Palmer's visit, not least because he had had to cancel his first appointment at the last minute. He did, though, telephone early in the morning on that day to say that he had a stomach bug and to ask for a further appointment the following week.'

'I see and did he turn up for that one?'

'Yes, he did.'

'Do you have the exact dates?' Sinclair asked.

'Hang on a moment and I'll get my appointments book, it's in that desk over there. Yes,' he said when he had found the page. 'His first appointment was on Wednesday 4 August at 9.30 and he arrived at the same time exactly a week later. 'He's a gruff sort of fellow, but, unlike a lot of people I could mention, the first time he did take the trouble to ring and tell me that he wouldn't be able to come.'

'What was his reason for coming here?'

'He told me that their mower had been giving him so much trouble that Mr Travers had agreed with him that the time had come to buy a new one and had asked him to look over a possible range of modern equivalents of both our walk-after and sit-on machines I'm surprised that they hadn't bought a new one before, because our mechanic, who went to service their old machine at the beginning of the summer, told both Palmer and me that the old one was bound to have a terminal breakdown soon.'

'Did he inspect your range when he came on the 11th?'

'Yes, he did and took a lot of trouble over it.'

'Did he express any preference?'

'Not exactly, but he did say that he wasn't getting any younger and that it was time he got a sit-on one.'

'What sort of price range were you talking about?'

'The cheapest sit-ons are well over a thousand quid, but even so, Palmer seemed reasonably convinced that Mr Travers would agree to buying one.'

'And did he?'

'I haven't heard from Palmer since, or Mr Travers, for that matter, but then I didn't expect to when I saw the news of the death of one of his daughters in the local paper. Looking into that, are you?'

Sinclair fixed his gaze on the man long enough to make him flush with embarrassment, then said: 'I'm sure you realize that we are not in a position to discuss anything like that and I would advise you to be very careful not to spread rumours of any sort yourself. Let me just say that we don't propose to leave any stone uncovered. Thank you for your help.'

Sinclair waited until they were out of earshot on the way back to their car and then said: 'That was inevitable, I suppose.'

'Yes, I'm afraid so. Not only that, I'm sure that the village must already be buzzing with rumours. I'd better give the press officer at the Yard a ring when we get back and I'm sure he'll give us a summary of what's floating around.

'The big problem, if we are seriously considering Palmer as a suspect, is his alibi, at least for the time of Alex's death, which seems to be absolutely solid, but I have grave difficulty in accepting that it was a stomach upset that kept him from keeping his first appointment here, when he had the opportunity to see those two Lolitas cavorting in the buff. If we're right about that, I wonder if he has previous form. I think it is about time we put Tyrrell in the picture, anyway, and one of us ought to do that.'

'Why don't you and I'll see if I can find out a bit more about Palmer. If he really did take photographs of those two girls, I reckon that he's probably done something like that before. My immediate thought is that Helen Rawlings mightn't be a bad bet as a start. She's lived here a long time and from what she's already told us, she's obviously been very involved with local affairs for a while.'

'Good idea. I'm sure you'd make a better job of that than me. Before you do that, though, why don't we check on Mrs Travers's next visit to Oxford, which I have discovered is tomorrow. I just don't believe that her account of the book club and lectures is the whole story. They are far too frequent to be credible and would hardly occupy the whole day each time.'

'I can see what you're getting at – that she might have a toyboy up there. If that has occurred to you, why do you suppose that Travers hasn't had the same thought?'

'Perhaps he has and doesn't care, particularly if our suspicions concerning his pliant assistant in the village are correct.'

'You may well be right and I agree that it's worth checking on her. If we're going to do that tomorrow, I'll see if I can fix a time to have another chat with Helen Rawlings on Wednesday. She knows what's going on in the village as well as anyone and I'd like to see if I can find out a bit more about Palmer, even though he appears to have a cast iron alibi for the time Alex was murdered.'

EIGHT

'**I** THINK IT WOULD be a good idea to use two cars,' Sinclair said over breakfast the following morning. 'If we use the in-car phone in the police car and your mobile in my mother's, we should be able to communicate satisfactorily with one another.'

'Why two cars?'

'It would give us more flexibility and if we alternate cars behind her she is less likely to realize that she is being followed.'

With the make and colour of Mrs Sinclair's car being unknown to Madeleine Travers, they decided that Sarah should take the lead to start with and she waited just within sight of the main gates of the Traverses property. Not knowing if the woman might be changing her schedule as she was only going as far as the outskirts of Oxford that morning, they arrived at 8.50 and waited with Sarah just getting a view of the main gates of the property and Sinclair some distance behind.

At 9.30, Sarah was just beginning to get anxious, when

she saw the gates swinging open and shortly afterwards Madeleine Travers drove out. There was very little traffic about until they joined the main road, but then there was a constant stream of cars and it was only at the expense of an irate driver sounding his horn and shaking a fist at her, that Sarah managed to slot into the line of cars heading towards Oxford. Twenty minutes later the car she was following swung left into a short section of road, leading to a large car park, already half full, situated in front of a collection of obviously new buildings. There was a super-store, a gardening centre, a filling station, a car tyre and exhaust fitting shop and an office block, as well as a partic-ularly imposing building, with an entrance above which were the words, WINTON'S RESTAURANT AND CONFER-ENCE CENTRE.

Sarah watched as Madeleine Travers walked towards it, carrying a large, leather case, then disappeared through the rotating door. She followed the woman a few minutes later with her hat pulled well down over her forehead and found herself in a spacious open area beyond. A number of black leather armchairs were set in front of the massive tinted windows, which were clearly designed to prevent passing pedestrians looking in, and several men and women were sitting there, all of them in business suits and with open laptops on the glass-surfaced, low tables in front of them. Some of them were conversing in low voices, taking sips from time to time from their mugs of coffee.

There was no sign of Madeleine Travers and, after waiting for a few minutes to make sure that the woman wasn't going to appear through the door with CLOAKROOMS in capital letters on it, she went through it herself, pulling her hat down even further, to make absolutely certain that the woman wasn't there, then went back to speak to the barman.

The man smiled and said. 'What may I get for you, madam?'

'Do you have a manager, here? If so I would like a word with him. My name is Sarah Prescott and I am a police officer.'

The man looked carefully at her warrant card and then said; 'Yes, we do. His name is Buxton, Raymond Buxton. I will give him a call.'

Only a few minutes later, a young woman wearing a white shirt and a black skirt with matching stockings and shoes came out of the lift.

'Inspector Prescott?' she said.

'That's right.'

'Mr Buxton will see you right away. If you'd follow me.'

She led Sarah into the lift and into the office on the third floor.

Raymond Buxton looked to be in his forties and got up to greet her. 'How may I help you, Inspector?'

'I understand that a Mrs Travers is giving a talk here starting at eleven o'clock.'

'Yes, that's right. She's with our projectionist, making sure that everything is in working order; that she knows how to operate the pointer and whether the video would be better in complete darkness or with some background lighting. Is everything all right, or is there a problem?'

'No, there isn't, but the reason I am here, is to make sure all goes well. I am sure you must have seen on the TV news or in the paper that her daughter was murdered only a short time ago.'

'Yes, and I was very shocked by it, too. I felt sure that Mrs Travers would either cancel her lecture, or at least postpone it, but she telephoned me yesterday to say that the best way for her to cope with everything that had happened would be to carry on as planned.'

'Do you know how long her presentation is going to last?'

'Yes, I asked her that and she thought about an hour, taking into consideration any questions and discussion. Were you planning to be at the lecture yourself?'

'Yes, but not in the auditorium. Mrs Travers felt that might upset her friends in the audience and she is not expecting me to be there. I am, though, reluctant not to be close by and I was wondering if there would be room for me in the projection room.'

'I don't see why not. When he's finished sorting things out with Mrs Travers, I'll introduce you to our projectionist.'

'Thank you.'

'Might I ask how you would deal with the press or any photographers who might turn up having heard about the event?'

'I think that unlikely, but there is backup outside and I do have this,' she said, showing her phone to him.

The man eyes widened slightly. 'I'm impressed.'

'Is your projectionist reliable?'

'I can reassure you on that point. He's not some young fellow out to make a quick bob. Reg Prentice a very nice and reliable man. He was head of the photographic department of one of the Oxford teaching hospitals for many years before he retired last year having reached the age of sixty. He was responsible for the television in the operating theatre and for all the photographic and projection apparatus there. He had several assistants, but did a good deal of the work himself. If you're worried that he might contact the media, I can assure you that he won't.'

'Excellent. I look forward to meeting him shortly and you're quite at liberty to tell him why I am here.'

Soon after Sarah had got back from reporting to Mark Sinclair, who told her that several women of roughly Madeleine Travers's age had arrived and there were no problems outside, she was introduced to the projectionist.

'It's very good of you to let me come up here, Mr Prentice,' she said. 'I promise I won't get in the way.'

'Don't worry, ma'am, but might I suggest that you don't say anything while we're live, because I am able to communicate to the speaker if there are any problems and we can, of course, hear what's going on down there.'

Sarah was fascinated by what followed. She was

convinced that Madeleine Travers had delivered the talk before, because she was very fluent, the whole talk flowed and she inserted some good stories. The various steps that the horses had to make were explained and illustrated by video with slow motion sections and the importance of the rider's posture was emphasized. She explained that hours and hours of training were required and that the rider's immaculate turnout and deportment was also vital. Any tension or unusual actions of the rider, even gripping at the wrong moment or with too much or too little emphasis could wreck the performance. The rider's relationship with the horse was closer, in a way, than any two people and the sensation when the two of them were working as one without fear or tension was indescribable.

She showed her winning performance at the European Championships and how devastated she was when her horse went lame before the Olympics in Seoul in 1988 and, although selected, she was unable to go.

After she had taken questions, the audience, small though it was, applauded enthusiastically and Sarah felt like joining in.

Once she had thanked the projectionist and the manager and had been reassured that the women were all in the dining room, she went out to the car and told Mark how impressed she had been by Madeleine Travers's performance.

'Considering the circumstances, it was quite extraordinary.

She must be a very hard nut indeed and it just shows how little she has been affected by Alex's death. She was fluent, funny in places and even though I had thought that I hadn't the slightest interest in any form of equestrianism, I was completely absorbed by it. Anyway, how about lunch; after all that I could eat, if not a horse, several of your mother's sandwiches.'

It was nearly two o'clock by the time the women attending the lecture started to come out and Sinclair put his hand on the catch of the driver's side of his mother's car.

'If I'm going to do a "peeping Tom" on Madeleine Travers, I think I'd better go in the police car as it wouldn't do at all to be arrested. After her performance, though, she might well give her other activities a rest. I'll see you back at my mother's house.'

'How did you get on?' Sarah asked, when Sinclair got back.

Sinclair raised his eyebrows slightly. 'How about a cup of tea and a slice of Mother's fruit cake and I'll tell you all about it.'

'Madeleine Travers was the last to leave the building and drove off towards Oxford,' Sinclair said when they were settled. 'The house she was making for was in one of a network of side roads and when the woman pulled up and parked half way along one of them on the left side, I had to pass her and get into the nearest slot, which was a hundred yards or so further on. Luckily, when I started to reverse into it, in my wing mirror I was able to identify the house, but not the person who let her in through the front door. There was a space on the other side of the road rather closer to the house in question and I decided to turn at a cross-roads a few hundred yards further along and was able to park.

'Although I could see the house in question, being a pleasant afternoon, what better, I thought, than to take a stroll past it on the pavement on the other side of the road. It was one of a row of modest terrace houses, quite small, with a tiny patch of grass on one side of the path and a couple of rose bushes on the other. I went further along the road for two hundred yards or so and as an old trot was coming out of the house I was just passing with her dog, I pretended to post a letter in the box further along, then came back giving her a smile as I went by. Surprise, surprise, when I was level with the house into which Madeleine Travers had disappeared, I noticed that the curtains in the upstairs room, which had been open when I had gone up the road, had now been drawn and I heard a sharp cracking sound, which was repeated several times shortly after.

'I settled in the car with binoculars at the ready and just over an hour later, two people came out on to the path outside the house. By leaning right over across the passenger seat, helped by a slight curve in the road, I got a good view of them through the windscreen. It was indeed

Madeleine Travers and her friend, who were engaged in a passionate embrace. The back of the latter was facing towards me and as I watched, Madeleine began to knead her partner's backside through the slacks with her hands. As they disengaged, I thought that the time had come to take cover and I was still crouched down below the level of the side window as Madeleine's car went by.

'Did you get a sight of her lady friend's face.'

'Not much of one, but enough of to be quite sure that it was a he not a she, and quite a young one at that.'

'Good heavens. Perhaps, Matthew wasn't making up his tales about his mother beating him after all.'

'Exactly and if all he said was true, then it's hardly surprising that he's so mixed up.'

When Sarah rang Helen Rawlings the following morning, she immediately invited her round for a cup of coffee and when they were settled in the conservatory, she listened attentively as Sarah gave her a summary of their thoughts about the case and their suspicions that Palmer might have been photographing the two girls, but that he appeared to have a cast iron alibi for the time when Alex Travers had been murdered.

'I know we are clutching at straws, but we are still not happy about him and wondered if you have heard any rumours about his behaviour in the past.'

'You mean peeping Tom stuff?'

'Yes and taking pictures of more than flowers.'

'Well, there have been hints about him, largely, though, about his possible interest in young boys, rather than girls and I remember mentioning that incident at the pub to you when you came to supper. He's always snapping away at the local primary school sports for the local paper, but that's always been with the permission of the head teacher and, knowing her, I bet she kept a close eye on him while he was doing it. Schoolteachers are hypersensitive to that sort of thing these days and if there had been any incidents, I'm quite sure she would have taken immediate action to get rid of him.'

'Has there ever been a village bobby here?'

'How stupid of me, I should have thought of that. Yes, there was, but when he retired some twenty years ago, he wasn't replaced. You could do worse than have a chat with him. You see, I do a magazine and book round regularly at the old people's home on the edge of the village where he's been since the death of his wife some ten years ago. Ken Price is a really nice fellow and even though he's in quite a bad way with arthritis and must be in his middle eighties by now, there's nothing wrong with his mind and he still takes an interest in village activities and gets to some of them in his wheelchair.

'He was sadly missed when he retired. You see, if there was trouble, he'd have a quiet word with those responsible and that would be the end of it. Now, you never see a uniformed man and we've had quite a bit of trouble with the young unemployed, who drink and take drugs. I'm sure he would be glad to have a word with you. If you like, I'll take you along there and introduce you to him. It's not all that far from here and I could do with a walk.'

'Thank you, what a good idea!'

'No time like the present. Drink up and we'll go right away. You won't want me hanging around when you talk to him, but why don't you come back here for a bite of lunch when you've finished and you can tell me how you got on?'

The old man proved delighted to see her and as Mrs Rawlings had said, he was as sharp as a needle.

'Weren't no women in the force down here in my day,' he said, then raised his eyebrows slightly and after a short pause, smiled at her and added, 'more's the pity. The girls round here are just as bad as the boys these days. I happened to read in the local paper about the girl who were drowned up at the Traverses house a week or so back; involved in that are you?'

'Yes and we're just checking on everyone who works there. We've already interviewed the domestic staff and talked to the gardener and his assistant, Phil Carter. Mr Travers obviously likes Mr Palmer and young Phil Rouse, but I was wondering if you knew anything about them as we don't want to start any rumours by inquiring at the local pub, for example.'

The old man smiled. 'You're quite right about that, hot bed of gossip that place is. I don't know anything about young Phil, only that he's the son of Bert Rouse. Right nasty piece of work he is. I had words with him once after he'd slapped his wife around when he was tanked up. That was not long before I retired, but I spoke to the landlord and one of his mates, who I knew a bit and asked both of them to keep an eye on him. From what I've heard he seems to have calmed down a bit now he's got older.'

'What about Palmer?'

'I first came across him when he was a schoolboy, 'cos he was always in trouble. There was nothing all that serious except the time he was suspected of being involved with a gang that set light to one of the ricks on old Mr Farrow's farm. I felt a bit sorry for him in a way, 'cos he had a brute of a father. Anyway, Palmer always had a way with flowers and when he left school, he started work at the local nursery.

'The trouble started when, in order to get better pay, he moved to a girls' school about twenty mile away from here and got a job as assistant gardener and general handyman. I remember it was called St Margaret's; that stuck in my mind 'cos that was my wife's name. If only the silly bugger had used a bit of commonsense, he might have done all right, but he was caught spying on a couple of girls, when they were sunbathing at the edge of the games field one Sunday and taking pictures of them. Judging by those of the flowers he took later, he really knew his stuff. Any road, the headmistress didn't want any publicity and all that happened was that he lost his job, got a police caution and I was told to keep an eye on him when he came back here.'

'Was there any trouble with him after that?'

'No and he was bloody lucky to get a job as gardener/handyman for old Mrs Forrest.'

'Yes, I've heard about her.'

'To give Palmer his due, he did a good job there. He gradually put the garden in order – it had gone to rack and ruin during the war when the military were there. He also used to help the housekeeper by doing the heavy jobs for her and Mrs Forrest wouldn't have a word said against him. After the old lady died, he was employed by the executors to keep an eye on the place and look after the garden during the time the property was up for sale.

'By the time Mr Travers had bought it, I had retired, as had Mrs Forrest's solicitor and I reckon the evidence of his caution must have got lost in the system. Mr Travers no doubt made some enquiries about him, but, whether he did or not, after a trial period he took him on as full time gardener and handyman. Palmer also looked after the motors, cleaning them and doing other simple things like checking the oil and tyres.

'It must have got a bit much for him as he got older, because Mr Travers took on Phil Carter to help him. He's a good sort is Mr Travers, everybody here likes him and he always gives a garden party at the house for the villagers in the summer.'

'What about the rest of the family?'

'Mrs Carlyle, his mother-in-law, involves herself in all the local activities and I've never heard a bad word about her. Like Mrs Rawlings, she does a trolley round here and always has a word with me and is such a cheerful person. It does me good to see her, but I've heard that her daughter, Mr Travers's wife, is a right Lady Muck. By all accounts, too, the daughter, the one who's just died, was a bit of a tearaway. I saw her at the fruit and flower show last year and she was a real looker. The lads and quite a few of their dads, who should've known better, couldn't keep their eyes off her. It didn't help either that her mother hadn't seen that she dressed properly.'

'Any idea what Palmer made of the girl?'

The man chuckled. 'I don't doubt that he'd have been snapping away at her in the old days, but I reckon he's too old for that sort of thing now and he just sticks to the flowers. By all accounts he's become a bit of grouch, always complaining about something, but he does keep that garden looking a picture.'

'How did you get on?' Mrs Rawlings asked, when she and Sarah were sitting in the conservatory of her house having their lunch.

'Mr Price is a delightful old fellow and he was very helpful.'

'Tell me about it.'

The woman listened in silence as Sarah related what the retired policeman had told her and then said: 'So the rumours about the fact that Palmer didn't confine his photographic endeavours to flowers have some credence.'

'They certainly have,' Sarah said, 'and I was thinking of trying my luck at that school.'

'Did he give you the name?'

'Yes, it's called St Margaret's and he said he only remembered it because that was his wife's name. He told me that it wasn't all that far away, from here. You don't happen to know anything about it, do you?'

'Indeed, I do and it's not such a wild coincidence as you might think. About ten years ago, our eldest son got a job as an IT consultant at a firm just this side of Oxford; our youngest grandchild, the one I mentioned to you earlier, is a day girl there.'

'That surely must be the one that Mr Price told me about. Have you any idea about the best person for me to approach there. I don't want to make too much of it, but it may just possibly be important.'

Mrs Rawlings thought for a moment or two. 'Last speech day there, I went to look at the archives department and I was very impressed by the woman in charge. She is a retired house mistress, I would guess about seventy, and is a real enthusiast. I'm quite sure that she'd be the soul of discretion, too. I'm pretty certain that she'll remember me as I spent an age there when I visited the department last speech day. You see, at that time I had been asked to give a talk to the local history society, about the development of girls' education in the nineteenth century and I'd heard that she was a mine of information on the subject, particularly, of course, related to St Margaret's. I gathered that she goes in every day and with any luck should be there now. Would you like me to give her a ring? I'm pretty sure she'll remember me and I'm certain her name is on my computer, as I retained the details of my talk on it in case I kept the promise to myself to write an article on the subject some day.' The woman gave a loud guffaw. 'Some hopes, as my ever tactful husband put it, when I told him about it.' She glanced at her watch. 'It's only ten to two so perhaps it would make sense to leave it for another twenty minutes or so.'

'Thank you, that would be tremendously helpful.'

The woman was as good as her word and after they had chatted about Sarah's job while they filled in the time, she rang the school and was put through to archives.

'Miss Price? Excellent, very glad that you're in. My name is Helen Rawlings and my granddaughter, Rebecca, is at the school at present. You may remember that we met last speech day and I pestered the life out of you over the subject of women's education. Now, the reason for my ringing you is that I have a detective inspector here with me, one Sarah Prescott, and she would like to discuss something that happened at the school roughly forty years ago. Let me say, at once, that it's nothing discreditable as far as the school is concerned. Any chance of your being able to see her this afternoon say at three o'clock, or thereabouts?' She looked across at Sarah, raised her eyebrows and then smiled when she nodded. 'Splendid. I'll give her directions.'

'I can't thank you enough, that's been tremendously helpful,' Sarah said when Helen Rawlings had rung off.

'Think nothing of it. I feel quite involved in this case and I know that Henry's quite worried about it, although he wouldn't admit it. It's not long before he retires and he is anxious not to make a mess of a potentially tricky case like this so late in his career, not least because the local MP is the father of the victim.'

Mary Price proved to be a slim, tall woman, with grey hair, who looked to be in her late sixties or early seventies and she smiled as she shook Sarah's hand.

'This is certainly a first,' said the woman when they were sitting in front of her desk. 'I've never had the opportunity to welcome a police officer in here. I am intrigued. Now, how may I help you?'

Sarah explained about Alex Travers's death by drowning in the pond at the family house and that she had undoubtedly been murdered.

'We have been talking to all the family members who live in the house and those employed by them. One of them is the gardener and I am currently checking his background. I understand that he worked here for a time in the past and I would be interested to know if you have any information on him.'

The woman nodded. 'May I have his full name and, if possible, the years he was working here?'

'Yes, of course. He is currently known as Fred Palmer and there is no evidence that he has changed his name. I'm afraid that I don't know the exact year as I didn't like to ask in the village. You see I don't want the man himself, or indeed the locals, to learn that I have been checking on him. I'm sure you know how easily rumours spread in small towns and villages.'

The woman nodded and made a series of entries into her computer. 'Yes,' she said, 'that wasn't difficult, I have it here. The name is the same. He was appointed in the Easter term of 1970 and he left in the latter part of the following summer term.'

'Have you anything else on him?'

'Only his age at the time, which was twenty, his home address and that he was the assistant gardener.'

Sarah looked over her shoulder. 'Yes, that's the man I'm after. Do you remember him by any chance?'

'Indeed, I do, he caused quite a stir here amongst those few in the know, of which I was one. You see, it happened on a Sunday afternoon during that summer term. He was caught photographing two of the girls, who were sunbathing in front of the trees at the edge of the games field. They admitted that they had been topless, but their housemistress, who was a friend of mine, told me that eventually she got them to admit that they were both more than that and up to no good, as she put it.' The woman looked across at Sarah and raised her eyebrows slightly. 'Excuse the circumlocution, but if one works here for any time, one gets into the habit of it. Anyway, the man doing the catching was Bert Adams, our rather crusty head groundsman. He was a very powerful fellow and not only did he collar young Palmer, but he ripped the film out of the camera, unrolled it and then flung both into the stream that runs behind the field there and marched the young man straight to the village policeman, a drinking pal of his, who lived nearby.

'As you can imagine, the headmistress at that time, Miss Baker, known by all and sundry as "the loaf", sprang into action and the upshot was that Palmer was sent packing and escaped with a police caution. The girls got away with a monumental telling off, had all their privileges withdrawn for the rest of term and were set to work cleaning out a storeroom. They were told that if there was any repeat of their behaviour, or if they told anyone what had really happened, whoever it was, they would be expelled and their parents given the reason.'

'And that was that, was it?'

'Yes, it was. You may find that difficult to believe with all the stuff one hears about the liberating effect of the sixties, but, believe me, there were no significant changes here until much later than that. In fact, a great many of the old traditions still hold sway and that has a lot of attraction for anxious parents.'

'So that was the end of it?'

'Indeed it was and, to tell you the truth, I am astonished to find how vividly I remember the incident, considering that I haven't given it a thought until today for so long.'

Sarah smiled at the woman. 'I am most grateful for your help and I'm sure you won't take offence if I take a leaf out of your former headmistress's book and ask you not to say a word about this to anyone, anyone at all. Our inquiries are at a very critical stage.'

'Don't worry, my lips are sealed.'

NINE

AFTER REPORTING TO Tyrrell, Sinclair spent some time with the records officer at the Yard without being able to raise any information on Palmer and got back to Oxford soon after one p.m., having had a snack lunch on the train. It was the exact timing of Alex Travers's death that was bothering him and he decided to pay another visit to the Travers house, in the hope of finding Mrs Carlyle there. He was in luck as, apart from the domestic staff and the gardeners, there was no one else in and she was free until she had to pick Lizzie up from her primary school at three o'clock.

'You may find this question a bit unusual,' he said to the elderly woman, when they were sitting in her small sitting room in her flat over a cup of coffee, 'but I was wondering if you knew anything about the watch Alex was wearing when she was drowned?'

'Indeed I do,' she replied.' I can't remember exactly what features it had, or how it works, but I do have the paper-work in my filing cabinet over there. You see, I gave it to

Lexie as a present for her sixteenth birthday, only a few weeks ago and although I knew she would look after it, I have to say that I wasn't so sure about the paperwork, knowing, to my own cost that those items have a habit of disappearing. So, with her permission I kept the receipt, the instruction manual and the guarantee.

'With characteristic acerbity, when she had seen the watch, Madeleine told me that I had been wasting my money, that it was far too good for someone like Lexie, who was always feckless and forever losing things, and if she didn't do that, she would be bound to drop and break it.

'I am used to that sort of thing from Madeleine and often let it go, but I wasn't going to do so on that occasion, particularly as for some months I had been taking more and more responsibility for looking after both Alex and Lizzie, for that matter, while she swanned off to Oxford, doing God knows what. Was she really just attending meetings the whole time, or was there another attraction up there? I had no solid evidence for that sort of innuendo, but she certainly became distinctly prickly when I made the point that she was hardly ever here and that although I enjoyed doing my bit, there were limits. She took strong exception to that, pointed out that I was living with them entirely at their expense and if I didn't like it, I could find somewhere else.

'I think she knew perfectly well that Richard would have had none of that and I told her so and it ended up with her storming out of the room. You may have noticed how frosty our relationship has been during the time that you and your colleague have been here.'

'What did she give Alex for that birthday?'

'A coat that was extremely expensive, but one that any teenager these days wouldn't have been seen dead in.'

'What about your son-in-law?'

'He gave her a gold signet ring and she was thrilled to bits by it, not least because a lot of the WAGS had been wearing them. She gave him a great hug and said that once she left school, she would never take it off. You see, jewellery of any sort is not allowed at Craven Park School.'

The woman shook her head. 'Enough of all that, let me get the stuff on that watch – it's in that filing cabinet over there.'

Sinclair studied the leaflet with care then said: 'May I take this away with me? It's just possible that further study of the watch may give us a useful lead.'

'Will I be able to have it back in due course? You see, I would like to give it to Lizzie when she is older.'

'Yes, of course, and I will taking personal responsibility for returning it to you.'

'I would be grateful if you would, because it has already crossed my mind that if I can get the watch repaired, it would be something later on for Lizzie to have as a memento of Alex. You may have got the impression that the two of them didn't get on, but that wouldn't be fair. There were times when Alex could be very sweet with her and my hope is that a little thing like the watch might in the long run be well appreciated when Lizzie is older. You see, I had a horrible suspicion that Madeleine might want to dispose of anything that might remind her of Alex. You see, in one of the rows we had been having with increasing frequency, she even told me that her adoption had been the biggest mistake of her life.'

When Sinclair met Sarah back at his mother's house late that afternoon, he listened intently as she described what she had found out both at the old peoples' home and St Margaret's School.

'Good work,' he said. 'That very clearly puts Palmer in the frame for Alex's murder.'

'I agree, but he seems quite literally to have a watertight alibi; and what about Matthew? We know he lied about his mother.'

'Yes, I hadn't forgotten about him, but first I'd like you to take a good look at Alex's watch.'

As she did so, he described how he had gone through the instruction manual, which Mrs Carlyle had in her possession, and what the information he had obtained from it implied.

'I think that the time has come for us to have another chat with Rawlings. I'll give Miss Ryle a ring after breakfast tomorrow morning to fix a meeting with him.'

'Good morning, Miss Ryle,' he said when the secretary

answered his call, 'it's Mark Sinclair here. Inspector Prescott and I need to see Dr Rawlings as soon as possible. A phone conversation would not be appropriate, I'm afraid. Any chance of this morning? It is rather urgent, perhaps you might tell him that we've got another lead in the Travers case.'

'He's got someone with him just now, sir, and you know what he's like about being interrupted, but I'll see what I can do.'

'Don't worry, I'll take full responsibility for it.'

'I've got another thought, sir. Might I suggest that you come here just before eleven o'clock? Dr Rawlings always takes a fifteen minute break at that time and I expect he'd agree to see you then, as it's urgent.'

'Thank you, Miss Ryle. We'll be there.'

To the detectives' surprise, for once the forensic pathologist greeted them with a smile.

'You certainly managed to put the wind up Miss Ryle, my dear Sinclair. Some dramatic new development in the Travers case, perhaps?'

'Not exactly, but we would like to take a look at Alex Travers's wristwatch. I take it that it is still here?'

'Yes, it is. All the evidence will be retained here until after the inquest. What, may I ask, can there be anything new to know about that?'

'Just an idea we had.'

'I think you'd better explain.'

'I will once we've seen the watch and perhaps we could also see a photograph of her left hand and wrist before it was removed.'

'Very well, but are you not going to tell me what you're getting at?'

'Not just yet. I need to check something first.'

'It had better be good, Sinclair.'

The detective wasn't in the least put out, giving the man a smile. 'Time alone will tell if that proves to be the case.'

Rawlings glared at him, then pressed the buzzer on his desk and, as usual, the secretary appeared with scarcely any delay.

'Miss Ryle,' he said. 'Something's cropped up and you'll have to reschedule my next appointment.'

'But what shall I tell Inspector Marriott?'

'That I've been called out on an urgent and important matter. For God's sake woman, he works only a stone's throw from here and anyway, he's bound to be complaining about something.' He looked across at the detective and glared at him. 'You'd better come up with something special, Sinclair.'

The detective wasn't in the least put out, giving the man a smile. 'Time alone will tell whether or not that proves to be the case.'

Rawlings was still muttering to himself when they entered the post mortem suite. 'Any special requirements before Evans gets the watch and the photographs and you get dressed up?'

'A sterile magnifying glass and a pair of forceps would be helpful.'

The pathologist sighed. 'You make it sound like a magic trick. Very well, but what you've got up your sleeve better be good.'

When the man returned, Sinclair scrubbed his hands and was then helped into the gown, mask and the surgical gloves by the attendant.

'I take it that no one has touched any part of the watch without using gloves from the time the girl was found.'

'No one here, but there's no guarantee that the boy who found the girl or the ambulance crew who tried to resuscitate her, didn't.'

'And has the watch been tested for fingerprints or DNA?'

'We saw no reason to do so as the watch was on the girl's wrist.'

'I see.'

When all the equipment was ready, Sinclair carefully lifted the watch out of the container, examined it through the magnifying glass and then, very gently, pushed against the winder with the forceps, nodding his head and then showing it to both Rawlings and Sarah.

'As you see, the second hand is now moving round and if you care to look at the face in a minute or two through a lens, as the letters are quite small, you will see that printed above the numbers five, six and seven, are the words "water resistant". That clearly is no idle boast as the watch is going quite regularly now. The winder has three possible positions. If pulled out to its full extent, the watch stops and the hands can be adjusted. In the middle position, which it was in when I first picked it up, the watch still remains stopped, but the date, which can be seen in the recess by the side of the number three can be altered by rotating the winder. Finally, as I have just demonstrated, if one presses it fully home, the watch starts again.

'If you are unfamiliar with the mechanism, you are welcome to try it out on my watch, which is sitting over there. It works in exactly the same way, but everything is on a larger scale.'

'My God,' Rawlings said, when he had done so. 'We've slipped up badly there by failing to have inspected the girl's watch carefully enough. The implications are only too obvious. The murderer must surely have stopped the watch, altered the hands and then left the winder in the stop position before returning it to the girl's wrist.'

Sinclair nodded. 'That's right and the only credible reason I can think for the assailant to have done so is to provide an alibi for himself. The fact that he was able to set up the watch means that he must have been familiar with that type of facility on it, but that in itself doesn't mean all that much, as it is so common nowadays and has been for some time. The possibility of some vagrant having come across the girl and being responsible for her death has been raised, but that, in our opinion, is a non-starter; such a person would have been much more likely to have stolen the watch rather than manipulated it in the way I have described. Very possibly, too, he would have tried to rape the girl, something which has been ruled out. You will no doubt have noticed that I keep saying "he" with reference to the murderer and that is because my partner and I believe that to be the case in view of what I have already said. We have no doubt, too, that he must be a pretty cool customer to have thought up that possible alibi on the spur of the moment. As to his motive, perhaps he was spying on her or taking photographs; she heard something, got up, turned to face him and that's probably when he hit her, most likely with his fist, knocking her unconscious.

'I can only assume that he noticed her watch, recognized its type and then realized that if he stopped it and altered the time on it, it would give him an alibi. Before that, though, he must have made a snap decision to kill the girl by pushing her into the water. We believe that there are only two credible suspects: Palmer, the gardener and Matthew Travers, who appears to have been jealous of the attention paid to Alex by his grandmother and the present she had given her.

'If one accepts that the time on the watch was put on it deliberately, either of them could have done it. Palmer claims only to have arrived at the Travers's property at 9.30

or thereabouts and was undoubtedly having a hot drink with the housekeeper at the time showing on Alex's watch. Making an alibi like that would only be credible if he was able to show that he was elsewhere at the time of her death, which is why we believe he altered the hands of the watch and left it stopped. No doubt he thought that no one would think that it was he who had done so and that they would assume that it had been caused by immersion in the water at the time shown on the face. Presumably, too, he waited by the side of the pond until he was sure that the girl had died under the water.

'My colleague and I have discussed this in detail together and in our view, the only person who had a motive and the capability of carrying out the action I have described, is Palmer, the gardener, and we know that he invited himself for a drink with the cook, covering the time he had set on the watch. We realize that all seems very calculated and elaborate and that it is unlikely that he would have been able both to think all that up and execute it so quickly. However, we reckon that there could have been twenty minutes or so between his killing the girl and approaching the cook.'

The detective peered at the watch again through the magnifying glass, paying careful attention to its back surface and the strap.

'I'm quite sure that you will want to check it yourself, Rawlings, but there is something of considerable interest here. There is an obvious crease on the leather of the strap at the level where its two halves were connected by the tongue of the buckle to fit the girl's wrist. However, there is a further crease, not very obvious to the naked eye, but clearly visible through the magnifying glass at the level of the hole above. That suggests to me that when replacing the watch on the girl's wrist, her assailant must have tightened it excessively and pushed the tongue through that hole. If the girl went into the water, say, at ten past or quarter past nine, that would still have given Palmer more than enough time to arrive outside the kitchen at half past when the housekeeper offered him a drink.

'I don't know how much fingerprints and DNA are affected by immersion in water, but as the back of the watch must have been pressed pretty hard into the top of the girl's wrist, perhaps they would have been protected by it and you might be able to find one or the other there.

'Have we got enough to charge him at this stage? I rather doubt it unless you are able to find any DNA or fingerprints on the watch. There may of course be evidence in his house, but at this stage I doubt if we would be able to obtain a search warrant.

'Why might Palmer have gone so far as to kill the girl? I think that's pretty obvious; having perhaps heard the man behind her and having caught him in the act of spying on and probably photographing her, the girl would surely have gone straight to her father about it. That would certainly

215

have been that as far as his job was concerned, not to mention a possible prison sentence.

'That's the bones of it and we were wondering if there was any possibility of finding any further evidence, such as fingerprints or even DNA on the watch.'

Rawlings shook his head. 'I'm afraid that I don't know enough about the effects of water on fingerprints or DNA to answer that question, but the case you have made for the back of the watch having been protected by the tightness of the strap makes it quite clear that we should check both of them out as soon as possible. Is this man, Palmer, your only suspect?'

'No. Travers's son, Matthew can't be ruled out entirely yet as he misled us about both his mother's and his own movements that morning. He fairly clearly did so to put suspicion on to his mother, but there might have been more to it than that.

'One last thing; the girl was given a gold signet ring by her father for her sixteenth birthday, recently. I noticed just now in one of your photographs the lack of sunburn at the base of her left little finger and I think it more than likely that she was wearing it that morning when she went down to the pool. Her grandmother told me that Alex had said that she wasn't going to take it off until she went back to school at the end of the holiday.'

Rawlings nodded. 'I might not have noticed it when I examined the body down by the pool, but it certainly wasn't on her when my assistant was preparing it here later on for the autopsy. Any further questions before we go back to the office for some refreshment?'

'No, thank you.'

Two days later, Rawlings rang to tell them that a satisfactory sample of DNA and fingerprints had been found on the back of Alex Travers's wrist watch, which were quite distinct from that of the girl and that they matched those of Palmer that had been found on the handle of the mower in the shed in Travers's garden.

'I think we've got quite enough to charge him now,' Sinclair said to Sarah, 'but I suppose we'll have to report to Watson first, not something I'm exactly looking forward to.'

To their relief, they discovered that the man had gone down with the 'flu and they rang Tyrrell at Scotland Yard.

'Yes,' he said, after Sinclair had explained the situation, 'I agree with you. I think, though, that it would be politic for me to contact the chief constable in Oxford and clear it with him before you go ahead. I'll get back to you as soon as I have done so.'

The two detectives heard from Tyrrell the following morning that he had got the agreement of the chief constable of the Oxford region and told them that they should charge Palmer and arrest him as soon as possible. They drove first to the police station in Oxford and then to the Travers house, followed by a police car with two uniformed officers in it.

The man was sitting in his office in the Travers's garden drinking a mug of tea, when he saw the two detectives and the uniformed officers approaching and he got his feet, standing at the doorway. He didn't react or say a word while Sinclair cautioned him, telling the man that he was under arrest for the unlawful killing of Alexandra Travers, that he did not have to say anything, but that it might harm his defence if he did not mention, when questioned, anything which he might later rely on in court, and that anything he did say might be used in evidence.

Palmer didn't make any protest, either, when he was handcuffed, led to the police car and driven to the station. He made no attempt to contact a lawyer when he was informed of his right to do so.

Later that day, the two detectives made arrangements to be shown, firstly and briefly Palmer's house by Reg Waters, the head of the scene-of-crime team and then all the man's effects that might have relevance to his trial, which had been taken to a secure store in Oxford the previous afternoon. The house was situated about a mile from the village and set back from a narrow country lane. It was constructed of Cotswold stone and had a thatched roof. There were two floors with the sitting room and a very large kitchen at ground level, two bedrooms and the bathroom above and a loft over that.

'The cellar is the area that will interest you most,' Waters said, when they had met him and were standing in the kitchen. 'It occupies the whole length and breadth of the building and access is obtained through a trap door set into this floor, which you can see over there. It was obscured by carpeting when we first came in and the trap door had a heavy duty padlock on it.

'You will notice when we go down there that it is quite dry. The heating throughout down there is controlled by that quite sophisticated, unvented boiler in the tall cupboard over there. It controls the temperature of the hot water as well as the central heating and over there, you can see an example of the radiators that are all over the house. I reckon this place must have been pretty damp at one time, but it certainly isn't now. It's clear from the papers that were found in Palmer's desk in the living room that the whole system was installed about ten years ago and he has had it serviced regularly ever since.'

'All that must have cost a tidy sum,' Sarah said.

'Yes, ma'am. Palmer's parents ran a honey business, which was very successful and when they died, he came into a good deal of money, enough to refurbish the house and purchase a lot of photographic equipment. Before I take you down to the cellar now, I'll quickly show you the sitting-room.'

'As you see,' the man said when he had opened the communicating door, 'he's got a word processor and a printer and has access to the internet. He has been busy at various porno-graphic sites and has downloaded a lot of material on to the library facility. You won't be surprised to hear that they mostly involve teenage girls taking part in the full range of sexual activities.'

'Any evidence that he's been visiting prostitutes or persuaded any girls to come here to have their pictures taken?' Sinclair asked.

'No, sir. He's been more of a peeping Tom photographing young people in cars or in farmhouse buildings. I mustn't give the impression that his photography has been confined to his voyeuristic activities; he has been taking pictures of flowers and wildlife for years and has albums full of them, some of which have won prizes. I've only flicked through them, but I found ones of fox cubs and badgers, which was enchanting.'

It was in the store in Oxford that they saw all the shots he had taken of Alex Travers over the years and also some of Lizzie. Some of them were innocuous with pictures of them playing tennis, doing cartwheels and hand stands and in separate albums were formal portraits of them on their birthdays and in family groups. Clearly he had been spying on Alex for years and, Sarah thought, by far the most porno-graphic were those of Alex and her friend, Rosemary, together.

Each picture had been stuck in with adhesive corners and underneath each one he had entered the details of the date they had been taken, the settings on the camera and the weather conditions.

The signet ring that Travers had given Alex for her birthday was also there and Sinclair had it labelled with instructions for it to be returned to him after the trial.

When they had finished in the store, Sinclair telephoned Travers's office.

'I have some important information to give you,' he said when he had got through, 'but I am unable to do so over the telephone. May we come to see you as soon as possible.'

'Is it that important?'

'Yes, sir it is.'

'In that case you'd better come here right away.'

The two detectives were shown in and after shaking hands with the man, sat down opposite him across the desk.

'We wanted to inform you in person as soon as possible that we arrested Fred Palmer this morning and he is in custody in Oxford having been charged with the murder of your daughter Alexandra. He offered no resistance, declined the offer of a lawyer and apart from that said nothing.'

'And you are convinced of his guilt?'

'We are not yet at liberty to tell you what the evidence is at this stage, because we cannot afford to prejudice his trial, but we are both convinced that it is both solid and quite compelling.'

'Do you believe that there will be the need for a full trial?'

'It is too early to say and it will depend on whether or not he pleads guilty.'

'My immediate reaction is relief that you have found out who was responsible for Lexie's death, but I'm sure you will understand that I and my family will need a great deal of time to come to terms with all this. May I say, even at this stage, how grateful I am for your efforts on our behalf and the courtesy with which we have been treated.'

Three months later Frederick George Palmer pleaded guilty to the murder of Alexandra Travers. He had continued to refuse being represented and throughout the brief trial, he said nothing apart from his plea and to confirm his name and address. He was sentenced to life imprisonment.